Jab I Met. . .

Jab I Met. . .

Sudhir Vinayak Joglekar

PARTRIDGE
A Penguin Random House Company

To order additional copies of this book, contact
Partridge India
000 800 10062 62
orders.india@partridgepublishing.com

www.partridgepublishing.com/india

Contents

Part 3 In School and College as a Student

Preface

My main hobby is to make friends.

I have made several friends at the most unlikely of the places.

I also enjoy telling stories.

All the stories in the following pages have been narrated by me... to 2-4-5 listeners.

But rather than 2-4-5 listeners, I thought "Let me make hundreds and thousands of friends, by presenting these stories through a book." The book, I thought, will help me reach out to all of you.

Hence the book...

Jab I Met... ...

(Note All the stories / pictures are a work of fiction and any similarity with real life / real people is purely a co-incidence.)

Special Thanks

I must express my profuse thanks to

1st Editor Muralidharan,

2nd Editor Yogini Joglekar and

Cartoonist Shirish Marde

for providing invaluable inputs for the book.

Without support of my family-members Shruti, Siddhesh, Sphurti, Dhanashree and Manohardada, this book would not have been possible.

Foreword

I consider it a great privilege to write the foreword for Sudhir Joglekar's book. Sudhir is my dear friend of many years and also my engineering batch mate. We go a long way in terms of knowing each other. But like in Sudhir's stories you will find that it has had many breaks and re-connects.

In our schooling years we were in the same locality and our residential societies used to have competitive cricket matches during school holiday seasons. These used to be no less in intensity than a league match. I don't have too much of recollection from those encounters on the field but it would suffice to say that those were competitive years.

We then met again (less competitive by then) during our engineering days at VJTI, Mumbai and were also hostel mates. Sudhir and few others of our batch mates were not just academically focused but were also keenly interested in various forms of art.

We graduated and went our ways but met by chance a few years ago at Bangalore airport. In the interim years I had realized the kind of edge the multi-talented /multi-faceted individuals have over the 'normal' academically focused folks. I was happy to hear and notice the significant contributions and progress Sudhir had made in the field of art and the profession he had chosen for himself. He had by then released a few successful movies in regional languages, TV serials and also many a reality show for a premier channel. He had achieved all these milestones, in addition to being part of the top management team of a large insurance company.

So, in a way, Sudhir has had his 'Jab I Met' moments with me too!

One of the key abilities of Sudhir in my view is his skill to weave many very interesting and meaningful stories from everyday events that we are or would have been part of, present the same in half-real, half-fiction style and drive home a message. Herein lies his strength – ability to draw commonalities between multiple conversations and present them dramatically. Like in the book, you will read about the story that he narrates about an office meeting and the 'unknown' silent participant, or about the time of his visit to Siddhivinayak temple and the link of logic and faith.

Sudhir's stories always have a connect to the present like the reference to the verdict of the (2014 Indian parliamentary) elections or take the case of the story 'On a good road to Bhiwandi'. The narrative in my opinion touches upon very many challenges in today's context. It's about passion for the job, it's about work-life balance, it's about 'power of mother's love'… maybe many more. Finally it's about how you view and create your own 'take away'.

Similarly when he narrates the exchanges between parents while waiting in the queue for a delayed flight, he touches upon the raw chord that we miss when watching the reality shows based on child artistes.

These are great examples of his ability to connect the dots and make the reader derive the 'appropriate meaning' from it. You could just read the book and feel happy or understand the underlying message - hidden and delivered in a package that is suitable to the audience. Is this what one refers to as the technique of delivering a strong message but adequately padded for soft landing? (To quote a famous Hindi ad line… 'zor ka dhakka dheerey se lagey…')

As they say humor is the ability to laugh at ourselves, at our circumstances. Humor gives us an opportunity to embrace our flaws. It thrives between our aspirations and our limitations. It diffuses conflict. It helps us cope with any situation at the very instant we are laughing. When we cultivate humor, we are letting go of other emotions: bitterness, resentment, or anger. Because, humor is truth.

Sudhir has used this humor, this 'rasaa' extremely well while penning these stories.

Through these stories I am sure the reader would be able to see things in a new light -- the foolishness of our preoccupations, the absurdity of our hypocrisies and of course, our propensity to see ourselves as the axis around which everything happens.

Wishing Sudhir the best and happy reading to all of you!

N Muralidharan
Bangalore

(N Muralidharan is an Engineering graduate from VJTI, Bombay University. He is presently operating as a leading Independent Executive Coach and lives in Bangalore. He is recognized by various industries' bodies for his contribution to Industry.

In his professional life he has held top management positions in Indian companies like Wipro and Modi Xerox and was also Country Head & MD for some leading IT US multinationals for their operations in the South Asia region.

He was one of the partners in the pan Asian job portal JobStreet. com which has operations in Malaysia, Singapore, Philippines, Vietnam, Indonesia, Japan and India. This was a venture funded start up and successfully got listed in Malaysian Stock Exchange in 2004.

Murali has been recognized for his accomplishments by various professional bodies and was selected as one of the **Super Achievers in India by Centre for Change Management and awarded the Indira Super Achiever Award by the Indira Group of Institutions**, Pune. He has also been recognized by Indian Institute of Materials Management as a **Distinguished Member for his contributions in the field of Supply Chain and Logistics.**

Since 2006 he has been involved in Leadership Development space across Industry segments and is an invited speaker at various events.)

Part 1

While I Was Travelling

I met these characters while travelling. I had to undertake several tours in my professional life. I met various interesting characters during such tours... I remember a quote by John Steinbeck.

"A journey is a person in itself; no two are alike. And all plans, safeguards, policing and coercion are fruitless. We find after years of struggle that We do not take a trip, the trip takes us."

For those who do not go on tours, it is always a matter of jealousy that some people get to go on tour...

But for those who go on tour, it is a fairly routine activity. It is only characters like Bajawat, Immigration officer, J.D., Janaki and Faisal who make such tours memorable. Every time I go on tour I keep looking for such characters...

But it happens only sometimes. Also you realize that this was my 'Jab I Met' character only after the interaction is over... If you get a feeling that you are missing these people in the daily walk of life then they fall into the...' (J.I.M.) Jab I Met character.

==

1

Bajawat and Parminder

WHO BECAME A MILLIONAIRE?

(KAUN BANA CROREPATI)

{He was telling me "It is all thanks to Mr Bajawat... Great man... He is no more... but before he passed away, he told me some of his secrets... those secrets and with my own hard work... voila..." My life was made (my life became Balle Balle)}

My secret ambition:

I must tell you that my secret ambition right from childhood was to become a multi-millionaire... (Multi-millionaire=crorepati in Hindi -10 million Rupees is 1 Crore)

As such, anybody who owns 300 to 400 square ft apartment in Mumbai is a multi-millionaire...

Thanks to my parents, I own a 350 sq. ft flat in Wadala, Mumbai and that way I am a multi-millionaire.

But what I mean is not that kind of multi-millionaire... I mean a real multi-millionaire... who for me is a KBC[1] inner or a *winner* in a horse-race or a lottery ticket winner or someone who makes it big through a business deal.

One such incident presented me with an opportunity to become a multi-millionaire...

The following narration will tell you who became a multi-millionaireand who did not.

---

[1] Kaun Banega Crorepati is a Hindi tele-serial based on Who Wants To Become A Millionaire

Sept. 01, 2013 Location: Roxy Cinema, Charni Road, Mumbai

Back from China, I rushed to Roxy cinema to watch the Hindi movie 'Chennai Express' and I was 10 minutes behind schedule.

It was Monday… The film had already crossed the Rs.100 Crore(Rupees 1000 Million) collection mark… and sadly, I had still not seen it.

I wondered what will Shahrukh (the lead actor) and more importantly Deepika (the lead actress) say if and when I meet them… Ha… Ha.

In a hurry not to miss the start of the movie, I almost rammed into a guy… a Sardarji… (a Sikh is locally referred to this way)

"Brother, a miracle has happened", He said,…

I recognized him to be the guy who was recently in my flight from Shanghai to Mumbai… but…

He had changed tremendously in last 21 days.

New diamond rings in fingers. Thick golden chain in the neck. I was wondering… how and when all of this had happened??.

If I remember correctly, he was a small time consumer goods shop-owner, who used to import some items from China every month and then sell them in India.

He was telling me "It is all thanks to Mr Bajawat… Great man… He is no more… but before his death he told me some of his secrets… I worked hard… and "My life became Balle Balle" … (my life was made)

I was surprised… at what Parm… (What was his name?)… Yeah… (I get it…) Parminder…

Parminder was telling me…

(In Flashback mode… 10th Aug night… Shanghai Airport)

I was on the last leg of my China trip and was at the airport to catch a flight and return to Mumbai… The time was 5pm…

for a 10pm flight to Mumbai via Delhi, I was quite early at the Air India counter…

There was nobody…

no staff, no passengers… slowly travellers were trickling in…

Most of the Indians with a sense of wonder in their eyes at what they had seen in Shanghai and also… with dejection written large over their faces.

obviously, because of the realization that Mumbai can never become Shanghai in their lifetime. This was not easy to digest.

Our Prime Minister. Dr. M.S. had promised in 2004, "Mumbai will be better than Shanghai", when the Congress government came to power.

Things were not so bad then… Now it is only potholes in roads, loopholes in the system…

some wise men say that even NaMo (Narendra Modi, India's new PM) with his magic touch and resolve can help only GenNext… not us.

7.15pm and then… there was some movement… slowly a queue formed. I was 45 th to begin with… I had lot of time to spare… so I had counted.

At no. 46 was a Sardarji who was short… abnormal for a Sardarji I thought he was not as well built as Sikhs normally are and at no. 44 was a bearded gentleman (French cut), wheatish complexion… Ht. 5 feet8 inches… watching me… and then watching his 4 packages… Not the usual air travel bags but two *'thailis'* (non- branded cotton carry bags) containing some powder, one cloth packing of something like rolled sheets… 'Bajawat'… he loudly introduced himself.

I shook hands… 'B A J A W A T'…

I had never heard of such a name in my life… But… may be… What's in a name? Our Chinese guide told us that his real name was Wong and American name was Mike.

As a chain - reaction I asked Sardarji [2] his name…

Parminder Singh… "I sell small consumer – items in Mumbai."

[This was the only interaction I had with Parminder before I 'bumped' into him at Roxy theatre…]

"From no. 45, when will I reach no. 1?"

… Surprisingly, counter numbers 1, 2, 3, 4, 5, 6 and then 7 opened. The queue started moving fast.

Chinese girls (outsourced by Air India) expressionless, mechanical… (may be hence efficient) were doing their job…

What's in the *thaili* of Bajawat? I was curious… and it is here that the drama began.

We were progressing fast.

At respective nos. 15(Bajawat) – 16(myself)-17(Parminder), Bajawat said to me…

"Things are very strict here… only one handbag and nothing more than 20 kg of luggage"…

I said, "OK"… not showing much interest.

We were progressing… at nos. 11-12-13, Bajawat made a comment on heat wave in Shanghai.

---

[2]   Sikhs are known as Sardarjis

I had to agree.

When At Nos. 4-5-6, Bajawat asked what brings you here? I said "touring".

"What is there to see in Beijing, Shanghai?… You should have gone to Hong Kong".

"but"… I said, "I have indeed been to Hong Kong". For the sake of courtesy, I asked him where he was from?

It turned out that he was from Mumbai and a businessman in wallpapers "I purchase European wall papers for my elite customers, but you see there are down-market customer too… for them I purchase something from China".

"I see".

The line was moving towards the counter. We were at respective nos. 1, 2 and 3… and when he was called at the counter, he thrusted in my hand one *thaili* (cloth-bag) saying "I am carrying two handbags… just hold this…

After I check-in and before you do, I shall take it from you… OK?"… He didn't wait for my reply.

However, in less than 30 seconds, I was called at a different counter.

I glanced over my shoulder… there was some argument going on about the kind of packing he had…

Now… within me, there was some difference of opinion between my brain and heart.

Heart telling me to help him and brain going against my heart… as it happens most of the time with me.

My heart was scared… and body was motionless… finally… my body moved taking orders from brain.

I went to Bajawat, and returned it back to him his handbag saying "I have my own handbag… sorry"…

I ran to my counter. I got my boarding pass… and felt relaxed.

After the check-in counter and after some time I saw him again.

He was in a room titled *Luggage Search Room.*

This time suspiciously that *thaili* was not with him… He started grumbling on seeing me.

These Air India guys are hopeless… See how they treat their Indian customers… and see how they treat foreigners!.

"What powder did the thaili contain?" I asked… "It had a bit of"… he wanted to explain…

but before he could complete his sentence accompanying his actions.

He was called in search room… he went in.

He met me again at the coffee counter after some time… Now he had a still different *thaili.*

Where did the first and second thaili go?

To satisfy my curiosity, I started the conversation walking with him towards nowhere in particular.

"Air India is a fantastic airline… while coming, they upgraded me to business class… because of overbooking…

(I had to be loyal to the Airline which was so magnanimous).

He said "Everybody is entitled to his opinion"… There was only disrespect for Air India in his eyes.

He changed his focus.

He asked me about my family… Upon knowing that my daughter studies in Chicago.

He said, "Oh… I have two nephews… one at Stanford and the other at MIT.

Besides, a friend of mine is professor at Harvard"… He was bent upon showing me he was one-up.

I realized I was losing the 'USA' battle… But.

I was not going to give up… "Forget USA, I have a friend in Dubai who controls 900 plus staff"

Bajawat: That is nothing… I have another friend who works in Australia, controls 1000 staff."

Oh… 1000 on 900?

"Ten on Nine" (Nehle Pe Dehla?In hindi)… So, now… This was becoming intercontinental… so many more subordinates than my friend?.

I believe smart readers like you know that when you are engaged in a game of one-up-man ship, you do/say all sorts of crazy things… Like.

He… "My friend has two swimming pools in his house… one indoor, one outdoor… Knows Bill Gates and Jeff Bezos"…

I… "Three swimming pools… one for him… the second one for the family and the third for guests… knows not one, but both the Clintons, also some Chinese Bosses"… (When you are in China, and bluffing, why forget China?).

After a while I was tired of cooking any more stories… He was not… He continued.

However, I wisely gave up saying, "OK… OK… you are better networked and have richer friends than I have… you win… I lose.

Now tell me what was in thaili no. 1 and then thaili no. 2… yes… yes… that pink thaili?"

But… Sometimes when you surrender so abruptly, other party cannot digest his success.

He did not answer… He was nervous is what I thought… It appeared he had not liked this question…

After a while, he was asking me in a hush… hush… voice.

"Do you really know a guy who controls 900 people in Dubai?… With a big house… swimming pools… who also knows Chinese bosses?…"

… I kept quiet… I was caught… The way we had described our respective friends, it could have been only Bill Gates or Warren Buffet or Shaikh of Dubai…

or people of such credentials…

Bajawat said," Listen seriously… I want to carry some chemical powder to India.

they won't let an Indian take it but in case your friend uses his connections or even phones.

I can *convince(patao in hindi)* these search guys… and it can benefit you also.

Not in Rupees but in Dollars… Millions of Dollars".

"And In India what will you do?"… I asked.

"If I can *convince* Chinese in China, is it so difficult to convince Indians in India?»

His confidence was amazing… but mine was not.

In fact, it was going downhill… almost gone…

Firstly I was still not able to figure out 'Who exactly that powerful friend of mine was?'

… But… At this mature age, I am quite a seasoned customer to maintain brave face and come out of such situations.

I said casually, "Why don't you tell your friend from USA/Australia?".

He opened his mouth… "I can't… look… he is busy organizing wedding of his daughter".

I had enough of it… *Arrey wah re wah!…* (meaning great!)

Your friend is busy organizing wedding of his daughter and my friend is playing marbles or what?… Not possible… I left the place… not feeling sorry that I was going to lose may be millions of dollars… "My friend is busy organizing weddings of his son and daughter both and also one funeral of a close relative"… I hurriedly left the place not bothering to look over my shoulder for him…

I felt great… 2 weddings and a funeral… (Like Movie '4 weddings and a Funeral') at Dubai…

ha… ha… Tell me (Dear Readers) frankly, who was one-up? Bajawat or I?

Where he went after that… no idea… In the final checked-in list of passengers… there was no name like Bajawat.

and then **On Sept 01, 2013**

Parminder was saying," Bajawat was trying to get a sample of chemical powder for his customer, an Indian company… Nobody helped him at check-in and Security… even you.

Finally with the help of local contacts… I sorted out the mess… It was just a sample of chemical powder… not drugs… I missed the flight along with him, but earned his friendship…"

After coming to India… the Indian Company tested and approved the sample… and placed order worth several millions of Rupees.

Bajawat could not believe his fortune… He had a heart-attack… and died… "one good thing happened" (*Ek hi baat changi hui in Hindi*)

He could not live happily but died... happily... out of happiness.

He shared with me all his secrets while dying... My life was happy after that...) *however*,... Some credit should go to you also!.

You refused to help him like 3-4 others... I used my local connections and explained to Airline people... Missed my flight for that... but...

but my life was made (*life ban gayee in hindi*)... like we say 'you made my day')Thanks a lot... *we will have dinner anywhere in the world as per your choice.*

This is my visiting-card... Call me any time..."

I was wondering... who was one up?

Even 'Chennai Express' was not going to entertain me now.

I learnt two lessons the hard way...

1) If somebody is boasting, let him... That is the only middle-class luxury we all can afford... Don't try one-up-man ship!

and

2) When fortune comes calling, which is not very often... welcome it... Don't argue...

... I won the argument with Bajawat but actually, it was Bajawat who was a million up... and... and... it was ordinary looking Parminder... *who became a multi-millionaire...* (crorepati)

============*==================*=============

2

Immigration Officer

HELPLESS AT DELHI AIRPORT!

{As always, I tried to joke. "Yeah! I look different in the photograph! But how to resemble the person in photograph? Neither do I have a spare moustache with me nor my company allows me to carry a personal make-up man to make me look any younger."

I was soon to realize that humour doesn't work with such officers…}

Location: New Delhi Airport
Time: **August 2013, 2nd week, 9 PM**

"You need to open at least one branch in BR_CS. (meaning Brazil, Russia, China & South Africa) In this directive from Finance Ministry (smart readers will know that blank space corresponds to India… some of us stay out of India so this explanation)

As luck would have it; I was that time location-hunting in China for our proposed Company-office, more specifically in Beijing and Shanghai. I was greatly curious about China, since I had never been there before.

I was near the immigration counter at New Delhi. On the TV at the lounge the Hindi movie 'Majboor'(meaning helpless, struggling) starring Amitabh Bachchan, Pran was playing… Old memories… watched this movie in Engineering College days… I remembered I was 'Majboor' for one full year in Engineering College before I could cope with the subjects and become comfortable… I didn›t like those technical subjects then, but I must confess that the same education has been giving me and my family the bread and butter even today… famous song from Majboor is playing… *Phir na kehena Michael Daru peeke danga karta hain…* (meaning 'don't say now that Michael is into a wild dance after drinking liquor') But I was thinking, "*Don't get lost in old memories… you must live in present. Old is gold, but it is also old…* There is an announcement. 'Proceed to immigration'… For last several years this has been one of the most routine activities. This time it was different!

The officer behind the counter looked like a typical Government officer… may be had just a year before retirement. He had a long, hard look at the photograph and then asked "Where is Sudhir Joglekar and who are you?" I mean I have been insulted, challenged so many times in government, municipal offices and elsewhere also… but I mean this was too much! My whole identity was at stake… Oh God!… Did I bring somebody else›s passport? I was apologetic, and sought his permission to look at my passport. Saved!… Thank God!… It was my passport of 2003 but had a photo with moustache. As always I tried to joke. «Yeah! I look different in the photograph! But how to resemble the person in photograph? Neither I have a spare moustache with me nor my company allows me to carry a personal make-up man». I was soon to realise that humour doesn›t work with such officers…

"*Do one thing. Get a new photo on passport stamped by Passport Office and take the immediate flight then… Passport office shall open Tomorrow 10 am.*" Now… then… passport office… that too at Delhi is not anybody's idea of spending time happily… what is to be done? I was wondering… but kept saying, almost pleading, "Sir, Please try to understand.

My hand reached into my pocket and it felt like 500 Rupees note and a visiting card… I had huge experience of tackling RTO police and wanted to start bargain with 100… *500 was too much to prove that I was I.* I have been a regular and faithful reader of various blogs and along with dirty jokes I knew the necessities of corruption by heart. I also knew it is wrong to indulge in such practices but depending on the situation, may be… only for this one time.

But wait… "For a little while let me try different track"… I thought.

Now after several days… I realise that for some reason good old film-actors Pran and Amitabh bailed me out of this. "Have you heard of Pran, the Movie – actor?", I asked.

He was stunned. "Was Pran's surname Joglekar?… may be his distant relative's?" Such thoughts must have passed his mind.

Outwardly he could only mutter… "Who doesn't know him?"

"*Have you seen movie Majboor*?", I asked.

There was a dialogue in his movie Majboor… when Amitabh says, "I have heard that government officers have their norms…" Pran says… But before I could complete… He interrupted… "You have heard it right… Only government officers have their norms… and procedures."

Then… Out came my PSU (Public Sector Undertaking) Company visiting card and letter indicating purpose of my visit etc. Now his face changed. "Are you going to stop PSU officer from performing his duty?" I asked.

Suddenly there was transformation in his approach. "Hey hey… I was just joking!".

I replied in most un-Amitabh like voice… "(Like say k… k… Kiran) "I knew it all along, you were just joking!".

Passport was stamped. I went to Boarding Gate and then onwards to China.

Now when I reflect back… what would he have done if I had mentioned the real dialogue?

I am surely not planning to go abroad that too via Delhi in near future… I am also hoping he (immigration officer) doesn't watch Majboor too soon.

(For those who have seen Majboor would realise what a mistake I had committed!… Substitute the word Government Officer with Chor (meaning thief) and that is the real dialogue in the movie… and now you will know… *I think in Life Sometimes you get plain lucky.*

P.S.

I narrated this incidence to my niece Neeta who came to India on holiday. Being from Chicago and being Obama's country-mate, she is convinced that her word will be final on all matters… I narrated whole story… Only change was that, I delivered Amitabh's dialogue in a deep voice. (At least I thought so…) She heard me out… Like most of the youngsters who are never easily impressed with their uncles… she said… to prove that you are you… you had to rope in Amitabh and Pran… *if you have to prove you are somebody else, just imagine what will it take? Can you manage that??*

==

3

J.D.

ON THE GOOD ROAD TO BHIWANDI

{"Yes, I work hard…
sometimes even on holidays… because I have lost too much time already.
when I suffered from paralysis. Besides, *there is another reason*"…
"What?" I asked.
"It happened 3-4 years back…"}

Till **September 2011,** things were simple… I stayed with my mother… To any direct question "I have a bungalow, a car, money and reputation, What do you have? "In Hindi movie Deewar style, I would answer," My mother stays with me! Meaning she is more precious than all the above."

This answer had power to neutralize any such insulting questions.

Whenever any character in a tele-serial dies, we say that the character is just a photo-frame now… By this logic, my mother went into photo-frame in Sept. 2011… and… after that, till I met JD on December 05,2013, I could never give any fitting reply to such insulting questions by others, (sometimes looking at mirror, I would even ask such a question to my own image)… "what do you have?"

And then… I met JD…

It happened like this…

Thursday, December 05,2013, 11 AM, in Scorpio[3] on road from Mumbai to Bhiwandi.

---

[3]   SUV brand vehicle of Mahindra & Mahindra

Storage problems are acute in Mumbai for any organization. Apart from digital storage, lot of physical storage is also necessary for a 94 year old organization like ours. Along with BSM(Bharat Shivaji Marde, Engineer,55) and JD(Jayesh Damle, 49, looks like a Military man because of mustache, walk and looks), I am on my way to Bhiwandi to select a godown space. People were comfortable in existing storage space at Andheri but economic reasons are forcing us to look at alternatives. 'Andheri can be used as a Sales office', is the logic behind this decision... Now for those who do not know Bhiwandi, it is an area full of textile units, a mix of Hindu-Muslim population, history of a major communal riot in 1984 but by and large peaceful after that... However the impression people have of the place is it is a little more plush version of Dharavi.

(The largest slum-area in Asia). With Mumbai real estate rates being what they are, companies are compelled to look for cheaper alternatives at places like Bhiwandi, even though it is not a popular decision with staff.

Loyalty is one virtue admired by our generation in India, may be also in Japan... Today's Indian youth treat their jobs most professionally, with no scope for loyalty... Contrary to this, JD is an extremely loyal person who has worked day and night for the last 27 years for our organization... He typically gets to work by 8 am and slogs till 7 pm. Add to that the work he completes additionally on Saturdays and Sunday too. (I was really curious about JD and his work-habits.) Senior to him both in age and rank, I am in a mood to tease and rag JD. While complimenting him on the long hours of work put in by him, I said, "I respect your dedication and devotion but according to some(surely me)," If you cannot finish your work in the office hours between 10 & 6, your efficiency is surely in question."

Sometimes to treat a wound, it has to be opened up. My words must have acted as wound-opener.»Yes, I work hard...

sometimes even on holidays... because I have lost too much time already... when I suffered from paralysis. Besides, *there is another reason...*

"What?" I uttered.

"It happened 3-4 years back... I had not telephoned my mother for quite some time and suddenly I suffered from a stroke of paralysis.

I was admitted to a big hospital in Pune.

They treated me for 6 weeks. The hospital bill was Rs 200K... (Rs. 200,000)

Everyday a new line of treatment... several tests, new interpretations, shock-treatment, experiments and several other means were tried, but to no avail. Sometimes the pain would be so much that, I would shout like an animal.

They would rush to me, give me a sedative, make me sleep.

After 6 weeks, I said enough was enough...

My relatives shifted me to another big hospital in Pune... 4 weeks of treatment... Same situation as in the previous hospital.

I wondered if the science of diagnosis had deserted the Doctors in these hospitals?... End of 6 weeks... Again, no result.

Another amount of Rs.150K was charged to my account.

Slowly, I was losing hope... so were my wife and son...

In her village, my mother was worried. Where is my son?... Where is he?... Why have I not heard from him?...

Whenever she tried to call she used to find someone else would pick the call and give evasive responses. Since she did not hear directly from me, she sent one of her neighbours to Pune… to check about my well being!

On knowing her 48 year old son's plight due to paralysis, my 78 year old mother (*I have not seen her, but the likes of her are present in huge numbers in India…* & the world!) got up from her bed… It was difficult for her to walk even 10 steps because of old-age…

but she managed and enquired about a Doctor near her place… a qualified (MBBS) person but a strange Doctor…

He does not have to practice medicine since he owns 70-80 acres of agricultural land and so… he enjoys kheti… (farming)

But he has developed a wonder medicine on paralysis and helps any patient who visits him… There are no phones in his dispensary… no receptionist… nobody is given an appointment.

(I suppose you can meet a lot of people by appointment… *not all*)

However, nobody who reaches dispensary is sent back… without being treated.

All the suggestions to open a hospital at a better place…. may be near the highway that were made to him, had fallen on deaf ears… All that he would do is respond by saying "I can earn money but I have a feeling 'once I commercialize', my 'siddhi'(Power) will vanish…" (May or may not make sense but this is exactly what that Doctor kept saying).

With the help of her neighbours, my mother arranged for a vehicle, took me to this Doctor one day early in the morning.

And kept waiting patiently for the Doctor…, as if she was fit and experienced no physical pain herself.

The Doctor came in by 9.30 am and examined me… Medicines which were all his own are given with an injection, nothing bought from a medical shop… And he said to me "Once this course is complete, you will come here walking on your feet after 21 days"…

Within 3 weeks, first time after 3 months, I could walk for 100 meters, it took 28 Minutes… and then… there was dramatic progress not arithmetic but geometric progression…

After 3 Months, I got cured completely… What medicines did Doctor give? only he knows!.

and How did I reach this Doctor?… only my mother knows.

Once again routine of daily phones of JD and mother started… Today she is well, tomorrow little weak, then some fever, again OK… Then frequency of phones reduced… till such a time, when a phone-call was received by JD to inform him that his mother is very serious.

JD remembered vaguely his mother complaining of asthma, chest-pain… But these were brushed as routine ailments of old-age… Hence no specialist Doctor was searched and no 'wonder'- medicine ever found.

Even in the last phone-conversation before becoming seriously ill," Take care" was what mother said as a parting shot.

Next day… JD reached his place and found that…

his mother was no more.

It was this guilt of not having spent 15 days or even 7 days with a lady who gave him birth and life, which sometimes makes JD uncomfortable…

"I cannot cope with this guilt and whenever feeling of guilt overpowers, I run to my office-desk and start doing work. I immerse myself in PC, files... whatever..."

Like the record-room being shifted from Andheri to Bhiwandi for economic reasons, for emotional reasons, I had to find a substitute or a mother no. 2. Otherwise... I might have gone mad!"

Sir, I treat Company as my mother No. 2 and rush to serve her... or even be with her in my difficult times... because..., *"A mother is not a person to lean on but is a person who makes leaning unnecessary..."*. (Dorothy C. Fisher)

On that good road(?) to Bhiwandi, It suddenly dawned on me... If need be, everyone can find his mother No. 2...

In his organization, in some hobby or in sport or in serving other needy people... whatever...

Thanks to JD, I got my confidence back...

To the sarcastic question of some dear friends," What do you have?" Now onwards...

I can continue to answer with my head held high "My *mother stays with me even now."*

(Mere paas ... maa hain!)

===

4

Janaki and Faisal

15 SECONDS OF FAME

{These TV folks would do anything for TRPs(Television Rating Points).

Reality show by Special Children? Some exclusive episodes? Add to that elimination every week… Oh my… Preposterous!… Weird!…}

A short brief…

This story is a tribute to some of my friends who take very good care of their gifts from God… also referred to by some as 'special children'

Location: Leh Airport

Date: Morning of 11th October 2013

I am returning to Mumbai after completing some official work… This is the story that happened between 9.00 AM and 2.30 PM. In the last four days, I was successful in commissioning a small office for our company at Leh, a beautiful place. Commissioning means… setting up infrastructure for an office… and starting the operations.

Two of my colleagues had returned back by the morning flight out of Leh and here I was… still at Leh.

The flight from Leh to Delhi was to take off at 11.10 am. In reality, when I reached Leh Airport at 9.10am, I was informed that though the Delhi-Leh flight had arrived; we should expect a delay, as it had developed a technical snag,.…

Could not do much about it... except blame my stars... (my colleagues were about to board their onward flight at Delhi for Mumbai. Again... *Could not do much about it... except envy their stars).*

Truth was that I had booked 11.10 flight so that my precious morning sleep is not disturbed. I had web-checked yesterday and had got seat 10B... middle seat... chance to look out of window gone, even aisle comfort was not possible now... Once again *could not do much about it!... except... blame my stars... But, I shall try again... to get a better seat.*

This kind of pushing everything on the 'stars' made me feel good... I don't 'do' anything and keep 'thanking' or 'blaming' the stars as the case may be... This solves so many inherent shortcomings many of us have... Like say... choosing wrong options... placing comfort above duty... making wrong decisions etc. etc.

The *'experts'* amongst the passengers were confident they would repair aircraft in two hours (such self claimed 'experts' can be seen in all walks of life... I had once asked a so called 'expert' how he became an expert? He answered me with a straight face... 'you have to declare you are an expert and world listens' (The world salutes powerful person.)

I was hoping that Leh-Delhi flight would take off on time... *but it remained only a hope. In reality,* passengers were waiting for aircraft to get repaired...

It was **11.10am,** the scheduled departure time but no change in the situation... Actually for another two hours, we had no boarding announcement.

All kinds of things that you expect under such situations started happening.

Like...

Passengers losing patience… raising various questions…

- What will happen to connecting flights?.
- What about people who had reached airport to receive their relatives/friends?
- What about appointments at Delhi and the business meetings planned for the day?

Passengers were upset but nobody expressed anger loudly… Understandable… To reach Delhi from Leh… only 2 options are available… 1) by air and… 2) by road… Again by road either via Srinagar [4]or Manali [5](a long and arduous 15 hours drive), both more than 400 kms away… What if they cancel the flight?

Better to keep quiet and not express displeasure loudly was the thinking of the majority of passengers… Stray ticket-cancellations were there… only to be absorbed by several wait-listed passengers.

Finally, **at 11 50am**, *security check* for Leh-Delhi passengers was announced… Not one to give up easily, I tried once more at the counter… any Window or aisle seat available?.

"Sorry sir" was the polite but firm reply… "flight is full to the capacity…"

"Madam, please try to understand… I need to take photographs… that's my job… if I fail, I could be fired"… Trying the sympathy angle… I was trying to make a convincing case (actually a lie) why I must get a window… but no luck today.

---

[4] Srinagar, Capital of Kashmir state, India.

[5] Manali, Hill station in Himachal Pradesh

Madam said," Please try to exchange the seat with someone yourself! We cannot help you much… <u>or</u> for a change, try taking photos from middle seat this time… Our airline will certify that these are photos taken from middle seat hence not very good. That would also cover up your limitations as photographer also."

After this *sweet* interaction… Again… *I had to blame my stars.*

Amongst the passengers were two special children, Faisal & Janaki, with their respective parents… They were about 11 or 12 years of age in my estimate.

They were not aware of what was happening… so engrossed were they in their own world that, they were asking for chocolates, tea etc and their parents obeying them… at least… outwardly taking orders from their children.

Along with a group of passengers I too got talking to them… *We learnt that they were going to Delhi to participate in a TV Reality show of all the things!*

These TV folks would do anything for TRPs (Television Rating Points)… Reality show by Special Children? Some exclusive episodes? Add to that elimination every week… Oh my… Preposterous!… Weird!.

Faisal, Janaki and their respective parents had never met each-other before but by now had bonded well…

About other passengers…

There were parents whose' *normal'* children had participated in such shows on TV… They narrated their experiences.

-Some child was made to weep in full view of the nation by commenting on his inability to compete.

-Someone was made to cry describing his family's struggle in meeting the ends... their livelihood depending on the a tea-stall that they managed back home.

- Someone was made to describe her father's accident.

Children who get discarded at these reality shows later on develop complexes... lose confidence and become psychological case-studies... They could sink into major depression if their performance is not considered up to the mark on a national platform.

Several academicians feel that putting kids under extreme pressure when whole nation has their eyes riveted on them, can be detrimental to their health... This emotional upheaval the child goes through is enormous and affects his / her psyche.

Everyone was sharing their experiences...

All of us were hinting at... in fact openly discouraging... the parents of Faisal & Janaki... from going to Delhi to participate in the reality show...

My study of special children was limited to movies like Rain Man, Taare Zamin Par(meaning Stars on Earth) and Marathi Dramas like 'Naati-Gotee'(meaning relationships) and films like Chaukat Raja(meaning King of Diamonds as in playing cards)... Schools in Mumbai like Dilkhush school... [6]... My opinion was that *God has made these special children, so that non-special people don't make a mountain of their small problems...* (Like... I was upset about not getting a window seat...)

---

[6] One of the schools in Mumbai for Special children

Around us, Faisal and Janaki… were doing what they felt like… and what they enjoyed the most… occasionally shouting at the top of their voice…

and the passengers were busy discussing pluses and minuses of their participation in a such a reality show.

In the meanwhile… finally the take-off is now announced for 2 30pm.

Airport Duty Officer Sukhwant Singh(Sardarjee) was a sensitive man… When it was announced that Leh – Delhi flight would take off only by 2. 30pm… He arranged his own car to take Faisal, Janaki along with their parents to the airlines guest house… Both Faisal and Janaki were now losing patience… not really comprehending meaningful words like *"Delays are an inevitable part of Life… Sooner or later, everybody will reach his or her destination."*. uttered by Dasbabu, a philosopher in the garb of a passenger…

Faisal and Janaki having left for guest house, only sensible, non-special people remained in the lounge… no shouting., no asking for tea or chocolates… outwardly at least.

I never thought, Faisal and Janaki were much bothered about participation in a reality show… But their parents… (like most parents) were a different lot altogether…

We were hoping they would forget the idea of participating in the reality show, when in guest-house they get time to reflect on all that we had said… but… an hour and half later… duty officer Sukhwant Singh sent his car again to fetch them (That also meant aircraft was now ready to fly!) and… all of them came back… All of us had questions on our faces... Why... Why are they doing this? However none of us asked this question.

There must have been some discussion amongst the two families at the guesthouse!

It was Faisal who answered our *unasked question* "WHY" when he said, *"I will appear on TV, keep watching for the date".* He had spoken on behalf of all 6 of them... Janaki's mother elaborated... *Normally, I neither complain nor explain anything... I appreciate concerns expressed by all of you but our life with our children is like... like... what you have seen here at the airport... In such conditions, we suddenly got an opportunity to participate in a TV show, thanks to a TV Channel... where not only our children can see themselves on TV, but also could get entertained... Accompanying them, we can meet so many other fellow parents who are in a similar situation like us... and learn from them, which otherwise we can never think of... most probably we will spend the remaining part of life on the sweetness of such memories... Is it wrong? Are they not entitled to '15 seconds of fame' like normal children? So what, if they have learning disabilities...*

Nobody had anything to say... Nobody could see her eye to eye because... we had no logical answer...

It was a moment of realization... To each... his/her own... Why should we get worked up about this?(Janaki's mother was a teacher herself and not just another crazy mother of a child artiste?)

Boarding announcement was made at 2pm... Faisal and Janaki were allowed to board first... While going through the boarding gate... Janaki's mother (as if she was memorizing a dialogue), said to nobody in particular, *"Delays are... just a part of life"*… Dasbabu who was standing nearby, corrected her, *"Delays are… inevitable part of life,* Madam"

(Dasbabu, possessive about his favourite philosophy, wanted his dialogue to be delivered exactly the way he did)… Janaki's mother paid no attention… She said again *"Delays are… just a part of life".*

Could not figure out just who was prompting her? Was it something inexplicable?

Two sentences were echoing in my mind…

1) *"(I will appear on TV, keep watching for the date")* "by Faisal
2) *"Delays are… just a part of life"* by Janaki's mother.

Faisal and Janaki entered the aircraft… I noticed that everyone got engrossed in their own issues… Connecting flights, who would receive them at airport?… Changes in their schedule at Delhi… so on and so forth…

I had my own big problem… *middle seat*… no window… not even isle-seat… My problem though frivolous and small, appeared to be more serious than everybody else's… one hour flight in a middle-seat… No photos? How is it possible?

After about twenty minutes and reaching the boarding gate the last… I asked at the counter… any chance of window or at least an aisle seat? Is there any last minute cancellation?

He checked, double-checked and said," yes. Three passengers got off the plane just five minutes back… You can sit on… Seat 18 A… Window seat… I can't issue boarding pass though… since they were already given their boarding passes…

So… finally, I got my window seat… can take photos… but was still wondering… Who got down)

Was it Faisal's family? or Janaki's family?... No idea.

I managed to take lots of photographs of mountains... Thanks... Thanks... whoever cancelled!...

I won't be fired now... Remember? It was my job... (Ha... Ha).

I was sure either Faisal or Janaki would make some noise in the plane and I would notice... But everything was happening smoothly and without noise.

What was it about '15 Seconds of Fame' that... Janaki's mother said...

At the airport after landing and while collecting the baggage... I noticed Faisal and parents... but not Janaki and Family... Faisal waved at me...," I will appear on TV, keep watching for the date".

I expressed surprise... and said to Faisal's parents, "So it was Janaki and family who got down... I had no intention to scare and make them cancel their seats... Faisal's parents were surprised, "What cancellation? Just postponement, sir... TV channel's Executive Producer called at the last moment when they were boarding the aircraft, saying that due to alteration in schedule, Janaki need not come today and can come day after tomorrow... since her group would be shooting only then... Faisal's group shoots tomorrow and Janaki's group two days after that.

Airport Duty officer Sukhwant Singh was a kind man... He gave them full refund as per rules and also arranged for three confirmed seats for day after tomorrow... Janaki is a sensible daughter of a sensible mother... she knows, "Delays are... just a part of Life".

For most of the parents, only inevitable (even non-negotiable)thing regarding their children is probably "entitlement to 15 seconds of fame". Some will get it tomorrow & some 2 days later.

P.S.:

I came to know later:
Shooting for both Faisal and Janaki was completed as planned.

It went well. *Both Faisal and Janaki performed well... though they were first timers! They were very happy in the company of other special children... God bless them and grant them their '15 seconds of Fame' and 'lot of sweet memories to their parents... to last a lifetime'*

All of us who wanted to convince them to drop the idea of show, could have become villains! Thankfully, that did not happen!

========*=========*=========*=========*========

5

Bollywood Superstar
at Siddhivinayak Temple
and *was astounded by mind-blowing political logic*

SUPERSTAR

{So, for arati of Hanuman people turn their faces to Hanuman idol… which is on the other side of temple… Superstar now faces us… I am in two minds… whom to watch? Lord Hanuman or Superstar? What a dilemma? *I can see Hanuman later… for now, Superstar it will be!…*}

Note/Disclaimer: 1) This is fiction based on some facts… 2) This is not a political piece though it mentions some political parties, people.

Siddhivinayak Temple, Prabhadevi, Mumbai is all about Ganapati and faith and what political logic has to do at temple? Purists might ask me!…

Also how can *logic be mind-blowing*? Logic can be a leveller… but mind blowing?

It is a contradiction, paradox… anything… some may say.

But… you see… the situation was so full of absurdities that.

I had to use this '*mind-blowing logic*' terminology… May be you will also agree when you finish reading this story.

April 06, 2014, About 10.30 PM

Just a while ago., India had lost to Sri Lanka in the T 20 World Cup cricket Match.

Earlier to this, Sri Lanka had lost four consecutive World Cup finals…

If India had won this World Cup, don't know what would have been the headlines in newspapers tomorrow.

But Sri Lanka won and this is what they might say.

"India floundered. *This is not the Yu(Yuvraj Singh) vi(we) know* … and all that.

But wait…

What will happen in the political field about 6 weeks from now?

Listen to this political algorithm or logic.

But, First things first.

We(me & my wife) are scheduled to go to Siddhi Vinayak temple on 7th morning... for the early morning Arati between 5.30 & 6 am...

Arati is a daily ritual, with live telecast daily on a TV channel...

It has become a great attraction for devotees and tourists alike.

7th April 2014, 5.15 AM

Reached Prabhadevi.

Parked my 'A Star' opposite to Siddhivinayak temple.

5.20 AM

For those who have visited this temple, they know that there are 2 enclosures for devotees... Enclosure 1 & 2...

Interiors of temple are such that from Enclosure 1(50-60 special people), Lord *Siddhivinayak can hear you even if you whisper.*

Whereas from Enclosure 2 (about 300 general people and nearly 15-20 feet away)... *you have to shout so that Siddhivinayak can listen to you...* what can be done, that's the way it is!

That means we have forced even God to have distinction between near-ones & not so near ones... very typical of human mind.

I entered Siddhivinayak temple and was in the to 2nd enclosure, jostling with the jam-packed crowd... Understandable... Hundreds of people... so many wishes... after all *very few genuine places you can go with some hope... Siddhivinayak is kind of... last resort!*

Soon the gates would close... No admission till about 6 am...

Luckily, there are lot of TVs... You can see Lord Siddhivinayak on TV, if pillars don't obstruct your vision.

Till arati began, I was observing and even got talking to some people standing close to me...

In the crowd there were several students; having completed exams and hoping to secure good marks and further on admission to good college for Medical, Engineering, CA, MS, MBA and courses like those t.

One couple was going to shift to Antwerp to join into the diamond-cutting business.

Boy's parents while being well-wishers also knew that next time their *Dikra (local slang for boy)* comes to India, he would have become a NRI having spent 180plus days out of India and then... God knows.

85 year old Dineshbhai was praying for his great-grand son to get admission in a prestigious school... Actually his son and grand-son had come yesterday I believe and Dineshbhai was there only to... increase the factor of safety.

There were candidates from all the political parties praying very hard... A candidate will win only if Lord Siddhivinayak supports him... (No place for merit, you may ask... well... well)

How did so many people confide in me?... I shall disclose... even though it is a trade secret... I declared... loudly... to no one in particular... *'If our house-painting gets over well within time, we promise Satyavinayak pooja to God'*... (painting work was to start at home later in the day)... These structural guys would laugh on hearing that I had come to pray for smooth completion of painting work... My daughter who is studying visual sensing also laughed... *While studying visual sensing techniques, has she left her common sense in India, I wondered.* But those who have got the painting work done, know what it is to paint room by room, turn by turn... day by day, week by week... It can be very messy... so feels my wife... so she was there... On hearing my confession, others laughed but also spoke their minds... So much for my trade secret...

Also secondly for me... Under advice of famous dietician Rujuta, I was successful in reducing 1.5 Kg in 3 Months... She had thought I would come down from 82 to 75 Kg but I am not a great diet person... In her *Chitpawan* (people who hail from Konkan region in India have this typical tone) nasal tone she had said.

Go to Siddhivinayak temple and restart the diet routine... May be God can help... So, here I was.

Can Lord Siddhivinayak with his famous big stomach solve my weighty issues?

Little paradoxical... some may feel...

5.32 AM

Why aarti hasn't started? Why? What are they showing on TV?

At 5.32 am, Enters a tall, very famous, well-known figure of Indian Filmdom... the Superstar and his family. They are treated as *VIPs* and are being accompanied by temple authorities. Now we understand the reason for the delay... But we are also delighted... What must have brought him here?

May be seeking Lord's wishes for his movie releasing on the coming Friday… (*Strangely it is about Ghosts and he is at Siddhivinayak… Lo… Kar lo Baat (take that)… For weight reduction and for the movie on Ghosts to do well, both of us have thought of approaching the great Lord Siddhivinayak*)

Or maybe he is seeking prosperity to family-members right up to his granddaughter…

All of us felt proud in the company of Superstar… star of the millennium…

Arati begins… and it goes like this… *sukhkarta dukhharta varta vighnachi…*

5.40 AM

After few Aratis, It is turn of Lord Hanuman (Indian Monkey God) Arati…

Between the idols of Lord Hanuman and Lord Siddhvinayak both the enclosures are located… So, for arati of Lord Hanuman people turn their faces to Hanuman idol… which is on the other side of temple… Superstar turns his face also… Now he is facing us… I am in two minds… whom to watch? Lord Hanuman or the Superstar? I can see Hanuman later… for now, Superstar it will be!.

Hanuman arati is over, people and also Superstar turn their faces again… to Lord Siddhivinayak.

Superstar has a… white beard… but his hair on the head is black!… God is great! So to become Superstar, this is a pre-requisite… Different colours… beard & hair… Noted.

5.55 AM

Aarti coming to close... Time to sing... *Om yadnyen yadnya majayanta deva stani dharmani... Rajadhirajay prasahya sahine...*

One lady circulates a plate(referred to as 'thali' locally) with flowers... Enclosure 1 people can touch these flowers, but from Enclosure 2 people, only front row people can touch... 2nd row can only touch shoulders of 1st row people... & 16th row touch 15th row shoulders... Everybody is happy... Next,... Niranjan thali comes... Same routine of back rows touching shoulders of their respective front rows follows...

Arati over... after taking Darshan (view of the Lord and the proceedings), people form queue to have teertha-prasad (divine water)... Devotees then come out of Temple... Even Superstar who has already had his darshan- teertha- prasad comes out... I want to say hello to him... but...

Some of his acquaintances meet him.

Superstar(SS): (deep voice) what's the matter, How are things(Kya haal- chaal? Sub theek?)

People of Group 1: all is well we were here because of election time.

(Theek hain... Bus, Election ke liye aaye the)

(There are some people who want UPA 2(the present government) to continue, since they benefited... Lord has to has to listen to both.(people who want change in power and to these folks too). Waving their *hands*, they left.

I moved towards Superstar but now, a 2nd group comes. They are cricket-lovers... in addition to being politicians.

Superstar (same deep Voice):

> India lost yesterday's match from winning position. (Kal ka match to India jeette jeette haar gayee!…)

People from Group 2: But what happened is fine. (*Lekin Achcha hi hua*)Both Superstarand me are surprised… even the other people standing near - by are surprised.

SS: Why? (only by expressions…)

P G2:

> In 1996Sri Lanka won the world cup followed by NDA winning with Vajpayee… Now after losing 4 finals, Sri Lanka has won world-cup… NDA-2 sure to win with Modiji… *the scent of the state of Gujarat (Matti ki Khushboo)* will spread all over India…

SS: Oh… (Superstar is now apolitical… So he only smiles. No expressions like when he says in Gujarat tourism ad… fragrance of Gujarat (*Khushboo Gujarat ki…*)

This logic had really stumped me… I could never imagine that Sri *Lanka winning the world - cup* would have such repercussions.

Inside the temple, we were under the spell of the Great Lord Siddhivinayak.

Now, out of temple some people wanted autograph of Superstar.

He politely declined saying…

If you have to take autograph… take HIS autograph.(Lena hain to 'unka' autograph lelo!…) I myself have come here for 'HIS' autograph.

His humility touches us… Voice is rich baritone and delivery perfect… I reflect and think its after all practice of several years which is coming through… Like say, "*Pawn moves only one house at a time, but queen can move in many directions & any number of houses…"*

Crowd is slowly beginning to disperse. Other priorities of life are catching up… Those who were late for arati and waiting outside, now want to enter.

After we come out of temple and I am on the road the distinction becomes clear.

-With the Lord, we had two groups: 1) Near ones & 2) Not so near ones.

Here on the road there are too many:

Superstar, his wife & grand-daughter went to their Juhu residence… in BMW.

His son & daughter-in- law went in their Land cruiser…

Several people went to bus-stops to catch buses after standing in a queue… & several other people walking towards the local railway station - Dadar Station… they have one last glimpse of the Superstar… Ditto with me.

So what if super star has disappeared, I walk towards my *A-star* and start driving to my company-residence at Dr. Deshmukh Road…

In the car I am thinking.

NaMo cannot win because of his decisive governance or e-Administration or Infrastructure development etc.

If at all he wins, it will be because Sri Lanka has won the T20 World Cup like they did in 1996.!

Like in the hindi song…

Jahan paonmein payal, Haath mein kangan, ho mathepe bindiya… (Where there is a decorative chain in the legs, a bangle in the wrist and a dot on the forehead)

It happens only in India…

Sri Lanka jeeta, Government Badla, Modi sarkar aaya,(Sri Lanka won, Government was replaced and Modi Government came into power)

It happens only in India…

Photos of of the Temple, the idol of the
Lord Siddhivinayak… below.

6

130 Strong Group

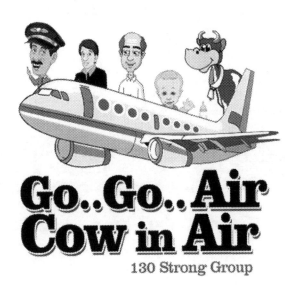

GO... COW... GOAIR... COW IN THE AIR

{"She was the 1st to get down and vanished to another aircraft to give milk to another Jyothi in another flight... She has conveyed thanks for giving her opportunity to be with the group & be of some use to them... This was translated in Kannada for one last time... By the Guide to a thunderous applause"...}

In October 2013

About 12 people from our Department had gone to Jaipur for All India Conference. Mumbai To Jaipur by GoAir (well-known low cost airline in India) was a very normal flight and 0n 19th Oct. we were scheduled to fly back o Mumbai. The incident narrated in following pages, happened during this flight.

We decided to try GoAir for its convenient timings. Once I had come from Chandigarh by GoAir and was happy. Why this name Go? I am always curious about how a particular name is arrived at? I was wondering... Was it Go as a verb?... Not to be confused with go!, the Hawaiian airline. is what wikipedia told... was it Go as in sanskrit language for a *cow*? what a weird thought? surely GoAir is not meant to be Cow Air... I hoped... I was happy with the joke of cow-air... Flight was scheduled to take off at 5.15 pm from Jaipur and we reached airport by 4.15pm.

Location: Jaipur Airport
Time: Afternoon, 19th October 2013.

When we checked in at Jaipur airport well in advance, we were told that Boarding gate no. 3 is on 2nd floor. On 19 th October, India - Australia Day-night cricket match was in progress. India were not in a good position and Captain MS Dhoni was trying his best to take India to a sound position. (eventually, he scored a 139 Not out and India 303 for 9, However, India lost the match, no thanks to James Faulkner who hit 29 ball 70 and was declared 'man of the match'.)

On 2nd floor, there was no TV and we wondered if we could wait on Ground floor itself, at least we could see Dhoni innings on big screen… But no luck… About an hour without TV… By the way, Dhoni had said in one interview he drinks lot of cow-milk… that is the secret of his strength… Is that why *he hits helicopter- shot so hard?*

Reached 2nd floor… It was very quiet on 2nd floor. There were few shops and people were busy making their last minute purchases. We waited for a while. Immigration counter was working hard to clear passengers for Dubai. Where was gate no. 3? Yes, behind the Immigration counter. We went there to wait for Boarding to commence. and… *the moment we entered that space*, it was a total change of scene!… So many families, children most possibly from South India, some of them were wearing dhotis, some Lungis[7](One person was actually showing lungi dance steps from *Chennai Express*[8] to 2-3 watchers… his friends and admirers. Various activities like "Catch me if you can", running, handicaps race with children

---

[7] Indian attire

[8] Famous Indian movie

jumping from each-other's baggage was in full swing. There was no sophistication of Airlines passengers what-so-ever... At its best it was a Railway platform, not 2nd class crowd but 2nd A.C. at the most!... On inquiries we found out that, it was a 130 strong group of a Fertilizer Company who were offered one trip per year with family... Bangalore to Delhi by Rajdhani Express, 5 days in Golden triangle Delhi-Agra-Jaipur. As a special feature, Jaipur-Mumbai was by air, GoAir and then from Mumbai to Bangalore by special Bus, dropping passengers on way to Sangli, Miraj, kolhapur and some places in karnataka on way to Bangalore.

Though boarding was to start at 4.45 pm, queue was formed right from 4.25 pm. For such a crowd, they are at their disciplined best when in queue... only because area of activity is limited by chains, separators etc.

Inside the aircraft, the same energy continued at a high pitch! Most of them were on their 1st ever flight to anywhere in life and excitement was very high. When it was announced that there will be 15 minute delay because of repairs on Run-way, it was greeted with a thunderous applause. Not that anybody understood English or Hindi, but there was a tour- guide whose duty it was to translate for the benefit of group... he translated in kannada, language leaving the announcer wondering what did she say to get a thunderous applause for a routine *delay announcement*... (This ritual of translating all the announcements in Kannada continued throughout the flight... even the oxygen mask announcement was greeted with cheers). Guide kept saying something in kannada... what was he saying? We were wondering but all his translations must be ending with something like ENJOY... After that a musical programme... cross between sa re ga ma pa(Do Re Mi...)and antakshari[9]... all sorts of songs were being presented with Gusto... Light switches, call switches were becoming a game of entertainment... if you could do it 10 times in 10 seconds, I can do it 9 seconds... Bets were being placed who would win? In the aircraft composition of passengers was like this... a group of 130 from Fertilizer company, 12 from our Company and some stray passengers who were totally outnumbered... They wore a lost look and could only hope landing at Mumbai was quick and safe... Flight took off and when it left the ground, it was again welcomed with a Vande Mataram... Will the flight end with *Jana Gana Mana?*... and it did exactly like that... Children standing on chairs... to prove that they also respected the anthem...

I was smart to book vegetarian combo dinner like 5-6 others in the flight ticket itself but when it was served to me, there were lots of jealous eyes... why only to him? *Is he someone special*? My neighbour, who was a technician in the Company, said in broken Hindi... anybody known to you in the staff? Lot of interaction was there on this topic... tension was mounting with people looking angrily at me... I requested staff to make some announcement that snacks for sale are coming shortly... the staff did that... and the same was quickly translated in Kannada... It was welcomed with fewer claps but there was some relief now... I could eat without much embarrassment...

A Snacks-cart entered from backside of the plane and everything was consumed in rows 24 to 30. there was unrest in rows after that... but they were told that within 30 Minutes

---

[9]   Musical game

we shall be landing and at Airport there are several counters serving different cuisines... translated in kannada, but no claps for a change...

I had finished my snacks and was feeling the need to communicate... that snacks were not too good... just ok... they had not missed much... not that I was too successful... I was in row 24 and in row 23 was a family of parents and 3 daughters... younger ones(Age 2and 4 approximately) were keerthi and Jyothi... so 6 year old could be Preethi... I mentioned Preethi to her father & realised I was wrong... Actually, she was Swathi... this little joke as to how I imagined a wrong name, was quickly circulated and if I could read expressions... it was something like... "so what you got snacks because of your influence... in terms of intelligence, you are nowhere compared to us!".

With a (false) promise of landing in 30 Minutes at Mumbai airport, staff had got good control over the passengers specially their deafening noise... and songs.

Everything was OK but Jyothi had different plans... it was her time to have milk and she started crying initially slowly and later on loudly... I had no idea a girl can cry so loudly for 1 cup of milk... the pursers assembled near our rows and somebody suggested to please give her milk... and buy peace. One purser said, "let me check!"... he went at the back of the aircraft and in 5 minutes really came with a cup of warm milk... he kept it in front of Jyothi... Jyothi managed to spill it twice making it half a cup... By now all the group had come to know that many things in the airplane were on sale except for influential crooks (?) like me... who were charged nothing.

Jyothi's father got up and asked "How much?" his one hand in Lungi's secret pocket... The purser said... nothing... he was virtually buying peace... with Jyothi... Guide and Translator of the group appeared... They wanted to know *why free*? Probably it was below their dignity to take anything free... In a tone of confidentiality, purser explained," There is a cow in the back portion behind curtain... since she gave milk *free*, I gave it to you *free*... Probably meant to be a joke, it was translated in Kannada by the guide... Entire aircraft was listening with rapt attention... but apparently, only the 130 strong group could understand kannada... Others may be swalpu... swalpu (meaning little bit). Narration complete... in a flash of seconds there was excitement, happiness of... getting to see a live cow at the back of aircraft... Like in a table tennis or lawn tennis match, when necks turn this way and that way... all the necks turned towards the tail of aircraft... some enthusiastic people opened seat belts and within a minute there will be race and commotion to see the cow first... nobody was bothered to listen to the purser, "But, I was joking!"... he mentioned about a cow only because what if 30 other children asked for milk? He would have said that cow had only 1 cup of milk... obviously joke had back-fired... Situation was going out of control... Group was about to get up and go... One alert staff –member informed the pilot, he grasped the situation and spoke in English... we are landing... all those who are standing, sit down!... otherwise we will have to open the doors and standing people will be thrown out... airline is not responsible!... when translated in kannada, it had magical impact... what is cow and a cup of milk, when it came to losing life itself?... peace prevailed once again... temporarily... Plane was really landing! But, after the plane landed, every passenger from the group wanted to exit by the back door, specially children... but where was the cow?

It was the National anthem break which allowed the cow to escape from aircraft without being bothered by her well-wishers (??) in the plane.

The purser explained, "She was the 1st to get down and vanished to another aircraft to give milk to another Jyothi in another flight... She has conveyed thanks for giving her opportunity to be with the group & be of some use to them... This was translated in Kannada for one last time... By the Guide to a thunderous applause.

All work and no play makes Jack a dull boy. *Seven days holiday in an year and escape from routine and reality appeared to have done wonders to workers and families.*

Cow was a fantasy and it was welcomed by them!

Normally, fantasies work with crowds, realities... only bother...

==

Part 2

In Different Situations, Different Locations… Practically Anywhere

(Page 121-133)

My Young Friends & Entry of Mumbai Monorail

Ravi, Vaishali Teacher & Anti-D Gang

(Page 108-120)

(Page 79-88)

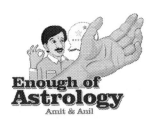

Enough of Astrology

Amit & Anil

I Shall Come Back! Special Gajendaran

(Page 97-107)

(Page 89-96)

Man with Many Names Chandan/ Manish/...

Talent for Absurd & Abstract NKB

In the movie *Anand*, character of Anand (Played by Rajesh Khanna) keeps looking for 'Murarilal' with whom he had shared beer at Kutub Minar, Delhi... Likewise I keep looking for my '(J.I.M.) i.e. Jab I Met...' characters.

I found some and some found me!

Not while sharing beer... But in several interesting situations... locations...

I met these characters absolutely anywhere... Sometimes at my work-place, sometimes at my home, sometimes in the articles/news items in the news-papers, on TV, in the Hindi movie land-Bollywood, on the first day when monorail rolled on made its appearance in Mumbai, the maximum city and for the first time in India, the most diversified country!

==

7

Special Gajendran

I SHALL COME BACK...

{Great heroes like Amitabh Bachchan, Arnold Schwarzenegger look very composed, determined and calm before they begin their fight – back (???)...
I had to begin my fight-back... here and now!}

*A*fter the Special Gajendran episode in our office, I was reminded of the Hindi movie Special 26 (2013) directed by Neeraj Pandey.

The movie '*Special 26*', takes its foundations from the robbery of 19 March 1987, when 26 people posing as income tax officials raided a jewellery store at <u>Opera House</u>, <u>Mumbai</u>.

In this movie appropriately titled 'Special 26' the story of these con men has been presented. The master brain behind these acts is the hero of the film Ajju and is supported by 4/5 associates, who pose as CBI or Income Tax Officers and carry out raids on shops, offices even at minister's residences and go scot free! The targets they had chosen belonged to the category, who indulge in what is loosely refer to as the number two business(not accounted in the books)!

@ our office: We recently had a unique experience. It was totally different from Special 26 but resembled it in some elements.

One day early in the morning in January 2014, I saw one of my colleagues Raman busy and in conversation with a decent looking, bespectacled gentleman over a cup of coffee. Raman offering coffee meant, he had a valued guest! I was right! Raman brought him in to my cabin! Being a senior officer, I was introduced to him. He provided me with a visiting card which read, Gajendran, Officer of Labour Ministry. He said he had come to carry out inspection at our site.

Never in my life had I this kind of visit conducted by such an officer from the Ministry of Labour.

'Inspection... Not just a visit', I was reminded by Mr. Gajendran.

I thought it was my duty to inform my seniors, so I took him to my senior, who said please provide him with all the records he desires. In a confidential tone my Senior added, I am quite aware that such surprise inspections are carried out! When executive at the level of General Manager tells me this, what could be done but to provide Gajendran with all the records?

Gajendran asked for copy of the work-order issued for the renovation work of the fourth floor at our Head Office and a list of all the contractors who are carrying out various works in our building.

Our staff complied promptly, though partially. Later I thanked them for not being too efficient... On the list was one Housekeeping contractor. He was summoned! Gajendran ordered our staff, "All the contractors whose offices are less than 3 Kilo meters away need to be called... beyond that, no need... I shall check everything myself and raid them if and when necessary." He made a loud claim. Long queue got formed of Housekeeping staff... Everyone was asked questions... How many hours do you work? What are daily wages? When are these paid? so on... and so forth!

Our department resembled a reality show-theatre... Gajendran sitting at one table like a Judge... One after the other participants entering, performing and leaving the stage… Between 11 am and 12 pm, I was away, attending some meeting and when I entered back my section after the meeting, the reality show was in full swing. I watched for few seconds, got a feel and sense of situation… Most of our staff had become spectators… and some were enjoying the show! I felt a bit of jealous too… because today due to this 'reality show', I missed the attention that I normally get whenever I get in or exit the section… Today nobody even acknowledged my presence.

My colleague Ravi quickly came to inform me that Gajendran now is asking for copies of documents *amongst them also 4th floor renovation work-order…*

That Gajendran had become the focus of attention was already bothering me and when I learnt he was demanding contract files I really became angry and mad to an extent. On what basis can he demand all these confidential documents… He had provided just a visiting card… there was no authorization letter… nothing to support his authority… I was losing my temper now.

Like Inspector Khan in Special 26… who would lose his temper at the mention of that gang of crooks. But no matter what, Inspector Khan was focused on nailing the crooks!

What will happen here in my department?? Can I do an 'Inspector Khan'

here? But firstly, was Gajendran a crook?

To tell you frankly, I am nice till I am nice, but once I blow a gasket, then… anything can happen! You can't even imagine.

I briefed my General Manager again and he was now serious. We went to the Director of our company and narrated him how some official from Ministry of Labour is asking us to furnish all kinds of confidential documents.

The Director grasped the situation quickly... There were no two opinions now... Director permitted me to tackle Gajendran the way I want to, except that keep your voice very soft...

From the first floor on my way to my cabin on the sixth floor, I went rehearsing how *softly* I needed to speak... People in the elevator, passages were looking at me like "What's wrong with him? No trace of usual charming(?) smile on his face, murmuring something, not even acknowledging courteous greetings. Has he become too big for his boot? Must be cut down to size... Let me do it. Why not right now?" With several people thinking like this, it was certain that one of them would pass some dirty, at least, sarcastic comments.

But... Hold on... looking at my walk... as if I was on some mission, people let me go without comments... Like they knew, *I am nice till I am nice; once I blow a gasket, anything can happen!.*

I reached my cabin... The moment I entered the department, the working up came to a halt... My gait and demeanor changed, I was cool now... 'Don't forget, speak very softly'... were the words ringing in my ears.

Great heroes like Arnold Schwarzenegger, Amitabh Bachchan look very composed, determined and calm before they begin their fight - back... From corner of my eyes, I glanced... Gajendran looked very engrossed in interviewing all those housekeeping contract labourers... I entered my cabin... Called all my colleagues, I thanked them for not being too prompt in providing all the documents and told them to 'withdraw all the co-operationone by one and in a very soft manner... Keep the tea service on... Take him out for lunch… but nothing about office… talk weather, TV, Politics; but nothing about work'… I was sure they would comply… and they did!… After all, company's reputation was at stake… In less than 3 minutes; every single soul from that centre – table position of Gajendran was gone… almost disappeared… Gajendran was left all alone… at the stroke of lunch… Potlekar and Chandra took him for lunch at an Udupi hotel… Gajendran wanted to go to our canteen to carry on with his inspection, but when it comes to obeying company orders, Potlekar and Chandra are extremely prompt and disciplined!… Together, they literally escorted him out of office… Lunch and then back to our department! No here… and no there!

In Executive lunchroom, news had spread like fire that our department was under 'raid' by some government authorities… Several advices were dished out!… *Why are 'you' tackling him? Send some seasoned contractor… Some of them were very keen to know how much deep trouble I was in?*… On knowing that it was inspection of our contractors, they were disappointed… "*Not directly but at least indirectly, are you not responsible?*" They wondered loudly. I said 'yes'… (Remembering devils have to be pleased first, Gods later!) But I added… "In an indirect manner, even our CMD and GMs were responsible, not only me! *Also, after my department, he is planning to visit all other departments too*"…, Now they realized the gravity of the situation… They were silenced completely and at least this 'threat' brought all of us on one side… Lunch over… "Please tell us if you need some help"… every executive told me… "Sure" I said. With the backing of our director, I wore that calm and serene expression of a saint and returned to my cabin…

2.30 pm... Gajendran's lunch was over... He came back... but no special welcome this time!... people were just doing their job... He called somebody, then another person... But nothing... no response... He decided to approach me again... I was ready... 'You have been searching for me everywhere, but I am waiting for you here!' can be a loose translation of famous dialogue from movie Deewar)

He must have realized something going amiss... when he opened his mouth, there was no arrogant, self- assured sound... he was realistic, "I wanted some papers?"

"Have a seat please", I said. My voice was so soft, he could not understand. He brought his ear near me, I took my mouth nearer to his ear and said, "Have a seat please" Soft but audible. (Bad Luck! At the same time, officer Ranjita entered. She could not interpret our respective positions viz. My mouth near his cheeks... She wanted to say something... but was too embarrassed... she went back. How to explain this closeness to her and actually what was I doing? I was thinking... (OK... explanations later... First things first)

As a result of my soft "Have a seat please ", he sat down. *First round for me!* Having drawn the first blood now I was aggressive but *not to forget, was soft.*

also. I said, following the rehearsed lines as much as I could," Can you produce your authorization? Who sent you here? We need it so that you can continue your business. Also please let us have in writing what documents you need!"

"No" Our department. doesn't issue authorization letters. There is no such procedure." Gajendran said.

"In that case we cannot part with any documents from our department. This is our procedure. I am not saying this, my competent authority is!" I said softly but firmly.

He shook his head as if he was helpless…

He took out a letter-pad and wrote. 'To check Implementation of Gratuity Act provisions please keep your records from 2010-13 ready.' He stamped it, signed it and delivered it.

I did not accept it. I made him deliver to inward mail department.

"Let's meet our GM", Saying this, I walked out of cabin. He did not follow me. Sorry! *I needed to be soft.* I looked back to him and softly repeated, "Let's go and meet the GM". This time he followed.

Looking at that letter, our GM said "Oh! This has nothing to do with your department. Send him to EWS department (Employee Welfare Scheme). I was later told by Potlekar and Chandra, that EWS people knew him well. Recognizing this regular customer of theirs, Senior Assistant Tanaji of that department said, "Please. take the officer to the godown and offer him cutting(half-cup) and special tea. I shall soon join."

Gajendran went to Godown to check gratuity provisions…

I was perplexed. What must have made Gajendran to visit our department? *Was he really carrying out surprise check? Or Had he simply exceeded his brief?*

In CCTV footage, it was revealed that there were two other people with him. Waiting at the 4th floor. My department people recognized them. They were representatives of the Contractor who had lost the 4th floor job by some margin. *Maybe* that's why he wanted to have copy of work-order so that he knew for how much the job was awarded?… also through all this drama, *maybe* we could have got scared and sent some contractors to him… to please him! Nothing of the sort happened, because ours is a PSU… About this issue of minimum wages, our lawyers have been vetting all the agreements thoroughly... No scope for any 'gadbad'... or hanky-panky deals in our Company.

In Special 26, a minister was raided by fake IT Officer / CBI officer, because he was having black money and never wished to lodge FIR... Same with the jewellery shops... they too had unaccounted items and cash.

I felt proud and thankful to our company... We may be going wrong in adherence to some of the procedures... here and there... little bit... But all the transactions are by cheque... or Electronic transfer of funds through bank.... No scope for unaccounted money here.

In our department, Potlekar (59), a very senior person went to see Gajendran off to the Elevator! People like Potlekar have been in the company so long... He commented to Gajendran to provoke, "Our Boss is a mad guy"(Hamara Saab pagal aadmi hai) But not me!. After you have finished work, let's have a drink in the evening!".

Gajendran was quick to understand what Potlekar was hinting at...

But he had realized his game was up, at least for this time... He declined asking "who is this competent authority?" Potlekar just smiled and waved him good bye. Gajendran said, "I shall come back! Some other time Dost, some other time." It sounded like a warning.

Well said Gajendran... People like you will always be visiting someone in some company at some point in time...

Based on this interaction, it was Potlekar and Chandra who started referring to him as *Special Gajendran!* So... then...

Till you come back and meet us again, Bye, Bye *special Gajendran*!

P.S.

In Special 26, Ajju the crook, returned by money order, the 100 Rupees he had taken from Inspector Khan saying," I don't rob money from honest officers."

People like Gajendran cannot harm you, if your systems are strong& you are straight-forward.

But, beware; *con men are two steps ahead of all of us*!

Hence, like they say (in Marathi),'Night belongs to the enemy! Always remain alert!"

==

8.

N.K.B.

TALENT FOR THE ABSURD AND THE ABSTRACT

{After a week or so, when I became somewhat experienced in tackling his question "How are you today?"
I would ask… "What are the options?"
"Good, bad, indifferent?" Remember, it was much before Amitabh Bachchan's tele-programme 'Kaun Banega Crorepati'… (Based on Who Wants To Become a Millionaire?) So options used to be only 3… not 4… Good, bad or indifferent?}

Time: 1985-86 approximately
Place: PSU Insurance Company, Properties department

Friends, this is a story of 1980s… I wonder how many of you *recognize* talent of the absurd and the abstract, as talent in the first place?… Some of my friends of present times don›t seem to be sure about this.

The properties referred to in the story have appreciated more than 100 times… how much more will they?… God only knows!

All the same, it should not stop you from enjoying this story.

I was working in a PSU(Public Sector Undertaking) Insurance Company in the properties department back in the Eighties!

For me, our company's properties department in mid-eighties turned out to be an interesting and hilarious place, thanks to my then *boss*… N.K.B… (N K Batliwalla) Since he was fond of addressing me as SVJ and others by their initials, we called him as NKB!

Aged about 55 and an Actuary by qualification, he was considered a very intelligent person by one and all and was for some reason posted in our department. (There was another Actuary in the Company and both of them did not see eye to eye, may be that was the reason) He used to wear a tie and... when he was engrossed in deep thought... and generating some (crazy) ideas... he kept on chewing the bottom portion of his tie. Amongst my friends, I used to refer to him as *tie-walla* in addition to NKB.

He used to come up with craziest of ideas... and I was the first person who would get to hear them. If I made a weird face when listening, *NKB would say "SVJ, what is life, if you don't have the talent for the absurd and the abstract?"*

After him, I have not met too many Actuarial professionals... I don't wish but certainly wonder, if all of them are like him?...

Right from morning our intercom conversations would run something like this...

"Good morninggggggg (In a sing song voice... meaning... 'How are you today?' Like song 'haal kaisa hain janab ka'... (Different tune like 'kya bolti tu'? meaning 'what are you talking about') Good, Bad or indifferent? (like a Hindi song say... like... kal mile ya parso? Meaning you wish to meet me today or day after tomorrow?)

Whichever way I answered, response would be the same... "Ha... Ha... Come to my cabin... lets have tea..." (like... Yahin... yahan koi... aata jata... nahin... meaning come here... nobody comes this way!')

After a week or so, when I became somewhat experienced in tackling his question "How are you today?"

I would ask… "what are the options?"

"Good, bad, indifferent?" *Remember,* it was much before Amitabh's tele-programme 'Kaun Banega Crorepati'… (based on Who wants to become a millionaire?)So options used to be only 3… not 4… Good, bad or indifferent?

Depending on my mood I would answer… Good… (40% of times…) Bad… (30%) Indifferent… (30%). After 3-4 weeks, I added few more answers… silly, crazy, awkward, wise, divine, fantastic… To all my answers, response remained the same.

"Ha… Ha… Come to my cabin… lets have tea."

What used to happen when we were having tea, could be described as *bizarre* to say the least… For about six months or so… till he was in our department… no morning conversation was normal and formal!

Sometimes he would say," You claim you are an Engineer… Right? (In Times Now's Arnab Goswami's [10] tone)

"Not only me, VJTI, Mumbai University certifies that… in fact nobody disagrees with that… How can you (disagree), Sir?

Ignoring my question… he would say "I have an idea!"… I kept on hearing his ideas (most of the times crazy) as a matter of routine, however later on, the moment he uttered these words, my heart would skip a bit.

I shall narrate to you one of the craziest conversations we had in that period…

---

[10]   Popular TV compere on channel Times Now

One morning, after the customary… "How are you?" in a sing-a- song voice and all that… He said," I have an idea.(My heart skipped a bit, now as a matter of routine)

NKB: "Have you visited our Malad [11]Staff Quarters?"

"Yes… a number of times…"

"What is your opinion about these?"

"Bad… Even Ex- Sheriff of Bombay and great architect Mr Bodhe has certified that… (Mr Bodhe was an 80 year old gentleman… a renowned Architect who became Sheriff of our city then known as Bombay… A giant of a personality… literally… and figuratively… I remember distinctly to have seen his passport which had 55 Entries to USA and back in those days…) Firstly, Malad Quarters are on a reclaimed land, with weak foundation soil… add to that lots of leaking walls… Secondly, the builder does not have great reputation… Thirdly… the builder has been absconding for a very long time…"

"Good… (Now… What's *good* about that? But such things did not matter to NKB)

OK… Have you visited Andheri Staff Qtrs…?"

"Yes…"

"What is your opinion on those?"

"Wonderful… In fact one of the best colonies maintained by a PSU…"

"I was wondering if you could do it?…" (NKB began nibbling bottom portion of his tie… danger signal… some idea was coming…)

"Wha… at?"

"Shift Malad Staff Quarters to Andheri…"

---

[11]   Suburb of Mumbai

"No problem… we shall issue vacation notices to all the people and shift them to Andheri…" I replied… but was wondering how could NKB ask such a straight question?

"Oh… that is very ordinary… I don't need a civil engineer to tell me that… What I am asking you is can you bodily shift the Malad Quarters to our vacant Andheri plot and implant it like a tooth… or like a plant in soil… If you can implant teeth… and plants… surely you can implant buildings also… If you can do it, then tell me what is the estimate?… Time 120 seconds… starts now…" (*NKB had assumed that I can do it!*)

"Now… to tell you the truth… Smart readers who know me know that I had enough madness in me to match his… at least that time… (Now I have become so-called sensible, mature and all that… At least I know how to pose like one but don't enjoy it that much) Immediately, I took out a calculator and after furious calculations, told him after 90 seconds…. Rs. 520million… plus 10 % contingencies"(It used to be a big amount those days…)

"Whaaat? Howwww?"

I explained that about 45 aeroplanes would be required to bodily lift all the columns, beams inclusive of foundations to carry the same through air… Add money for municipal permissions… police protection… Renting out aircrafts, third party liability insurance… repeated visits to Boeing and other aircraft manufacturers… all over the world etc.

There could be some income also… Once we decide on the date of shifting, we can advertise and can charge one rupee (may be more) each to all the people who want to watch this show from terraces, roads, gardens… the more strategic the location… more the charges… (I maintained a deadpan face narrating all this… any moment I could have exploded with laughter…)

Not much amused at my 90 second solution, his bespectacled face was now showing signs of getting disturbed... but on the face of it... he said... "Ok... put up a proposal and report... we have to take *Board approval...*" He also complimented me later," Surely you have talent for the absurd and the abstract... you are more than a match for me... I can get transferred now... Baton is yours now...

I guess he found it too much to convince the Board about cost of Rs. 520 million plus 10% contingencies... He decided not to pursue the proposal.

"At least let us appoint a committee" I requested... but he had taken a decision...

I was just lucky that he did not insist... otherwise I would be standing in front of the committee convincing them about all this crazy stuff.

Management must have realized that NKB was too intelligent for this department, so they transferred him... May be NKB wanted it like that!.

Till the end... or more precisely, till he got transferred... on several occasions I could never understand *whether he was joking or whether he was serious?*... His face was innocent and childlike and offered no clue but there used be a faint smile at the corner of his lips is what I remember now.

Decades later... In 2009... By chance, happenstance, co-incidence, whatever, but I occupied the position and chair of NKB in the same cabin.

Like King Vikramaditya's singhasan[12](throne), this talent of absurd and abstract grips me sometimes... I narrate some crazy ideas to my young engineer direct recruit friends... and

---

[12]   It is said whenever King Vikramaditya would sit on a particular throne, qualities of Judge would be imbibed by him. Likewise,

keep watching their responses… But… to tell you the truth… Neither I can generate those crazy ideas on a regular basis… nor can I be as innocent as NKB… Also… nor do I get crazy responses from them like I used to give…

"There is clearly dearth of talent for the absurd and abstract" NKB would have said.

Today's engineers in our company are very intelligent, smart, more focused in their careers as compared to us for sure, but… There are no replays here… these guys are very serious types… very limited moments of unadulterated fun…

NKB passed away in 1990… Several people remembered and appreciated him for his brilliance and eccentricities… so, I was not the only one to appreciate him!

I am still waiting… one day that crazy officer may still come… who will reply me tit for tat… baton has still to be passed to the next generation… not only of absurd and the abstract but of unadulterated funny moments even in a target - oriented, tough and dry place like our office.

Times have surely changed… can't say… for better or for worse?… sorry…

I mean… for good, bad or simply indifferent!.

Apologies*: There is complete mix-up of eras and times… e.g. I have used TV programme KBC of 2000 and some songs of Nineties to describe conversation of Eighties… But smart readers know that movies, especially Hindi movies (which is my staple diet), rarely had logic as their strong point…*

==

when I sat on NKB's chair, qualities of 'absurd & abstract' would be imbibed by me.

9

Chandan / Arvind / Manish

THE COMMON MAN:

IN REAL LIFE AND IN REEL LIFE

{Because, Movies cannot entertain me… Dramas are very expensive… Reality shows are all I can afford… was his response!

So far I was taking pride in the fact that from client's side, I was involved in a good, creative project…

And there was this common man for whom, this was just a Reality Show…}

(Those of you who have seen movie Rangeela (colourful)[13], would remember the character of 'Director' played by actor Gulshan Grover, who keeps saying, "My Films are not for Indian audience! I make films by Hollywood standard!"

This movie has some very interesting scenes like…

The heroine has no time for listening to the story / dialogues. When heroine's mood changes, her mother calls "Pack Up". The director is frustrated and asks in desperation, "In Hollywood there are no mothers hanging around heroines. *How can great movies be made with this type of mothers around?"*

In another scene… He requests Production Manager to provide him with a bus…

The Production Manager who is out to cut costs, asks the Director can he manage with Auto Rickshaw?

---

[13]   Successful Hindi Movie of 1994.

Director gets furious... How can you expect me to make a good film when I have to work with rickshaws as a substitute for bus? What I need is a Bus... a Bus...

There is Urmila and Aamir, Jackie Shroff [14]and other characters and a (footage-wise) minor character of a *common man* in the midst of the crowd which has assembled to watch the shooting of the film... Not many dialogues... for this character... Only expressions...)

Location: Renovation Site.
Date: Jan. 02,2014

When we, the three of us. Bharat (Engineer, 50), Bhushan (Engineer, 25) and myself went from Mumbai to Pune for renovation of our Divisional Office at Laxmi Road (in one of the busiest of the roads in Pune a 6000 sft (600 Sq. M.) of commercial space). All of us were excited at doing something new, creative... possibilities of a good project...

Chief Architect Dixit was unwell and there was his assistant Rakhi conducting the meeting...

In the meeting, the following people were present... our company officials, Architect Rakhi, contractor Prashant... There was also a man with a leather jacket, moustache and sitting on a pile of Vitrified Tiles... Looking like... like... may be the Security Supervisor of the Commercial Complex.

For some reason he had a batch "Chandan" on his shirt-pocket... He had a cigarette on his lips... not a real one but the mint- type like say... the brand Wills...

---

[14]   Urmila Matondkar, Aamir Khan and Jackie Shroff are important Indian Movie actors.

12.15 PM. Meeting started.

"I am looking forward to a great project"... I sort of made the opening remarks and set the ball rolling... Budgets, Approvals... what new accessories can be tried?... Everybody participated... but not *Chandan*.... His face was expressionless, not very unfriendly though... At about 12 30pm, the Secretary of the complex (in which our office was located) came... and asked the contractor why his labourers were drunk while unloading tiles late at night at 12 30am earlier that morning?

"Sorry... Sorry... these Pune labourers are... not like disciplined Mumbai labourers... I could find only these people at that time of the night... Tiles had to be unloaded in the night itself... I never knew they will drink after getting the work... Sorry... Won't happen again." Prashant Said.

(What am I hearing? *Mumbai labourers don't drink and are disciplined? One big revelation*)

For the 1st time, there was some expression on *Chandan*'s face... Like, he disapproved the comment on Pune labourers... But the matter was not much further deliberated... Everyone just left it at that... For entire hour and a half, *Chandan* was sitting there... on the boxes of tiles...

Only one or two changes of expression which I noticed...

For some reason, Rakhi was very bookish... perhaps, it was her first big project... no... no... not perhaps... surely... first project was for a Bank and second was ours... but size of our project was bigger... She read out rules to the contractor...

Rule No. 1: *Your supervisor has to be available all thro' the day...* I shall pay a surprise visit anytime... contractor Prashant having tackled several projects asked,

"What if my supervisor has gone to the market when you make a surprise visit?

Rakhi insisted," No… He has to be present"… There was deadlock in the discussions…

The text books in the course of PMC(Project Management Consultancy) never mentioned such possibilities.

Bhushan intervened… "Perhaps, cell phones can be used."

Accepted… first minor dispute resolved!

One by one, several issues came up for discussion.

12.45 PM.

Tea was served with biscuits… I became more curious about *Chandan*.…

"Mr. *Chandan.*, are you from the contractor›s side?

"No"

Till today, I have not perfected art of asking open ended questions.

So I ignored *Chandan* and the project discussions continued…

For some reason, Rakhi was under impression that the client(our company) is also a bank like her first client… May be the Chief Architect did not brief properly.

"*If the bank approves*" was her standard phrase… I had to clarify… *We are not a bank*…

But like some dialogue which an actor has learnt by heart… she kept repeating 'bank' for 5-6 more times during the course of discussions… We kept correcting… *We are not a bank… We are an "Insurance company"*…

There was very little humour apart from this… On 7th attempt, she got it right…

If «*Insurance Company*" approves…

Bhushan corrected… "no… no… madam, *bank, not Insurance Company*"… So, now it was my colleague Bhushan was the actor who missed his lines…

I *realized, when a lie is told emphatically several times, it sounds like truth… Now… I noticed Chandan having a faint smile on his face… (The smile appeared to read like…*

'Now why not try correcting your colleague?"). But Bhushan was quick to realize… sorry again madam, *"Insurance Company, not Bank"* Rakhi looked at me triumphantly… I was the client and I pretended not to notice this dialogue…

All the while… my curious eyes continued to be focused on *Chandan*…

I asked him, "Are you from the architect's side?"

"No." his reply.

One word again.(How to get into a conversation?)

1.15 PM

There were some other points…

Chandan was expressionless and quiet… Did he agree? Did he like/understand what he had heard? Did he not like?

Can't say…

Oh… Got it… It suddenly stuck me… May be, he is from the commercial complex… Such types are from property offices…

When the meeting was almost over, *and a good project had taken its first few steps*, I focused my attention on *Chandan*.

Me: What's your name? *Chandan*?

Chandan: No, My name is Arvind… *Chandan* is just a name
    on the batch…

Me: Oh! You are from the complex?… Right?

Chandan. / Arvind:… No…

He replied, bringing conversation to the dead-end… in just one word.

My imagination was working overtime now…

Who was he? A Thief?… Taking note of the materials on site?

But why he will expose himself so obviously?

I just came up from the road by stairs… (*You can only come up from the road by stairs like all of us… or climb down from the terrace like thieves*).

I see… I was thinking, "How to phrase *'Just who are you and what are you doing here?'* in those many words and yet… sound decent?

But he himself put forward his side of the story… "I am just a common man!".

(This common man is back in fashion today)

"Member of AAP – Aam Aadmi Party- Pune Branch, is it? If so, then, Where is your CAP?" Bhushan asked.

(All common men had to be members of AAP was his belief.)

"No. Since Pune is hot at 1 pm even in January… It is better to be in shade under the roof… rather than moving on the streets…

Additionally where else can get a good entertainment like your meeting?

I visit several such meetings all over Pune city… sometimes to renovation sites like yours… each and every day… at least one per day…

I never knew there was some meeting here… It was just a chance"…

Why do you attend meetings? I asked.

Because, Movies cannot entertain me… Dramas are very expensive… Reality shows are all I can afford… was his response!

So far I was taking pride in the fact that from client's side, I was involved in a good, creative project…

and there was this *common man* for whom, *this was just a Reality Show…*

BACK TO… Movie Rangeela

In the movie Rangeela, When the Director shouts *how can I work with a rickshaw when I need a bus?*

There is a *common man* who is in the crowd which has assembled to watch the shooting… He sympathizes with Director… no words… Only by expressions… When this happens twice again… with Director shouting, "how can a good movie be made in such conditions?" and the common man sympathizes with no words and only expressions…

Director wonders," who is he?" and orders that this *common man* is to be told to quit… No place for such onlookers in shooting!"

Switching back to our project site…

But this was not shooting of Movie Rangeela… It was our renovation site…

I was about to shout at Chandan / Arvind and order him to quit the scene... But, I controlled myself... somehow, I had enjoyed his presence...

"Surely your name is not Arvind... What is your real name?"

"My real name is Manish"... He had no hesitation telling his new real name.

"Can I see your I - Card?"

"Sure. (But he did not show his I-Card)...

Only when I am sure of the credentials of the person asking my name, I tell my real name...

I have attended hundreds of such meetings... Only twice, I was required to reveal my real name...

Usually, nobody notices me... Even If they do, they don't ask questions... and even those who ask questions, don't ask for my identity card... People are so busy in their own thing/ selves, nobody bothers me...

There are only some people *like you* who have an eye for detail... According to some people, "The God is in Details!..."

I wondered, Was that a compliment? But outwardly said, "Thanks. God may be in details... I am not too sure but I am sure your real name is neither Chandan, nor Arvind nor Manish... Actually who are you?"

"Why do you want to know the truth? "(C /A /M) said.

"B*ecause God is in truth and not in details, and the truth is in I-Card, not in what you say...*"

"If you insist, I shall tell you my real name... Where do *common people* have names to boast of? They only exist... That's all...

He handed over to me the I-Card... in an envelope... Inside, It was a valid Motor Insurance policy of Our Company... premium Rs. 550 /-

So *he was our Customer... small but valuable.*

Should I read the name on Policy??

It was M... something... not legible...

I returned the policy... still not sure about the name... *Some mysteries are best left unsolved...* For sure, he did not look like a thief or a shady character... "*What's in a name? We only exist... that's all.*"

This man (C/A/M)was adding to the mystery...

I thought, "Let the mystery remain... Enough to know he is our customer- meaning God."

Back to Project Discussions:

People were reviewing the bar-chart detailing the activities of the project progress. The great thing about our company projects is that *come what may,* they get completed somehow. It is like the great Indian Wedding, with all its challenges they get conducted well in the end.

Climax of movie Rangeela is reached & Urmila becomes a big star; but in real life, if there is no common – man, who will watch the movie?

Likewise, this renovation project hopefully will be a good project, divisional manager & other staff will bring millions of rupees of business, satisfy customers, service the clients... one thing for sure... next time when I conduct site-meeting in Pune, apart from the usual characters in the meeting... unless and until, C / A/ M is there, it won't be interesting... I suppose.

Two observations:

1) *Meeting may be conducted but will not conclude properly!*
2) *Without customer how will project take shape? and what's the point in doing a project?...*

==============*=================*=============

10

Amit and Anil

ASTROLOGY? NOT AGAIN!

In the future, I am not going to act as an astrologer… even by mistake.

{I keep looking for real stories in life and I did not know at that time, but here I was about to become a part of a story. I am normally prepared to hear anything on such occasions: But… I must confess I was not ready to hear what I heard that day…}

In about next 10 Minutes,

I f you believe in supernatural, you may enjoy this story. However, if you don't believe, please note that…

1) This story is based on real life incidents… and…
2) The supernatural does not care, whether you believe it or not…

So relax and read the story… You might enjoy!

August 2012

1)

"*Big and Important*"… does it sound like "*Rich and Famous*"?

May be. One thing for sure… Most of us aspire to be *Big and Important (B and I),* irrespective of how we spend our day-to-day life…

One opportunity to be *"B and I"* came recently in my life... But.

what a turn it took!...

Well... It happened like this.

It was an evening after a long hard day at a client-seminar.

All the colleagues were relaxing in the evening over a few drinks...

A 30 minute folk arts programme just got over and we were about to retire for the night and I was looking forward to a good night's sleep.

I accompanied my colleague Mandeep Nayyar from Ludhiana, Punjab to his hotel room...

I said "good night" but since Mandeep was a little high, he stumbled on something and just in time I helped him from falling flat on the floor...

I asked, "Are you alright?"

Mandeep said, "Yes... and No... Yes... because you *held me just in time* and no... *because you can't help me much in real life"*.

I got a little perplexed and I asked him to explain his answer.

In the afternoon in the client-meet, I had spoken about...

VUCA world (Volatile, Uncertain, Complex and Ambiguous) and how to tackle it through high quality Risk-Management... techniques... of course stressing about the insurance products of our company!

It looked like Mandeep was referring to that and wanted to tell me something.

I had time and Mr Nayyar had a *real-life story* to tell me.

"Do you know anybody in Singapore?"

"Hmm... Why?"

"I shall tell you"… Mandeep started speaking.

I keep looking for real stories in life and I did not know at that time, but here I was about to become a part of a story.

I am normally prepared to hear anything on such occasions: But…

must confess I was not ready to hear what I heard that day.

Just two years ago, Mandeep (50) Senior Divisional Manager from Ludhiana, had distributed sweets…

His younger son Amit was studying at one of the top engineering colleges and had completed 2nd year successfully… 2nd rank… and now his elder son Anil had received admission letter to one of the top management Institutes… the best of the Institutions in India… as per Mandeep.

I had heard that Anil travelled from Kozhikode to Mumbai on motorcycle in two days and today… Mandeep was asking me do you know anyone in Singapore? This is what had transpired… Since Anil did not get a satisfactory campus placement, he opted out of that and found a decent offer from Quizcraft (Event Management Company, name changed)… Initial training was at Singapore…

However to his horror, when he reached Quizcraft Tower at Singapore, he was not even allowed to enter, stating they do not have any intimation from their Bangalore HQ.

Bangalore HQ clarified that no recruitment letter was issued to anybody by the name, Anil Nayyar… Sadly, to beat competition, Anil had paid money to some unscrupulous character to get a decent placement… as if, h*eavens would fall if he lags behind his batch-mates at College…*

… Anil was camping in a nearby hotel and visited daily the Q'craft Tower in the hope of… getting started somehow with the training…

If Anil's story was shocking, Amit's was pathetic…

I could not decide which story was more heart-breaking… Anil's or Amit's?…

Amit's neighbour at the engineering college was placed with *Facebook* after the last round of selection of 1 out of 2(Rs. 7.2 million per annum)… Needless to say the loser in the last round was, Amit!

Amit was later placed at a workshop… probably a start-up at Allahabad… not bad, per se… but… can anyone face his parents when the dream of Facebook HQ at Menlo Park, CA is shown… and when you wake up, all you get is some workshop at Allahabad…

Complete mismatch between aspiration and reality.

Amit was taking sessions with a psychiatrist… After placement was announced in 7th semester, Amit refused to attend classes in 8th semester.

Amit's mother had to camp at the college campus to keep this boy motivated to complete his 8th semester.

Mandeep said he and his wife were not able to come to terms with their VUCA world!!

He quoted what I had said in the lecture… "Most difficult to manage are one's expectations…"

And he requested me to *help him in his problem.*

I told him there are two options how I or anybody could help him…

Option 1) Young generation does not need any advice. Just believe in them… remind his sons to "Be brave and Tough. On every step you will encounter difficulties. Courtesy Hindi Movie Tezaab "*Learn from Life. Life teaches everything. It is your test, Why punish Papa?*")

and

Option 2) To be proactive and help him saying "I will not shy away from responsibility!".

But how?

Mandeep was thinking… and suddenly said, "Yes, you can do it. I want you to be *proactive*"

Mandeep clarified… I know you can act a bit… *I wanted to take objection to the word 'bit" but kept quiet…*

"You are an *astrologer*… I mean you have to act for some time as an astrologer… famous, learned but not much known in Mumbai… In fact you are on your first visit to Mumbai… »

"And then?" I asked. (Apparently, Mandeep wanted me to be proactive by actually acting a part of the role of an astrologer)

My question *"and then?"* convinced Mandeep that I was getting into the role of… an astrologer.

Words were echoing in my mind If one can't use his art/craft for social good, what's the use? I always enjoyed playing Big and Important and… here was an opportunity…

After he explained everything about Anil and Amit…

their CV, details, plus and minus points… How Mandeep's 50 year old eyes viewed both of them… What he wants them to become?…

Anil to become a Loss Adjuster… Since Mandeep's friend has made it big in that position.

and Amit to pass UPSC exams… and join Government Department… a Big House… Power… Status… etc.

I said, "O.K. Tomorrow, Let them come at 10am sharp… Less than 30 minutes is all that I require!.

(*to give a new direction to their life*)"

"I will send them at 10 am but please ensure that you make them wait… a good 30 Minutes at least…

Remember, Important people are never on time… They come late… but can show the people waiting, that they are early…"

"Let's see about that… Being an officer, I am not comfortable with delays anywhere… Specially from my side…"

Mandeep, "This is a good opportunity. Polish your skills to act Big and Important".

(Mandeep knew that to act '*B & I*', was my necessity and also a weakness.)

What could I say?

How was I going to tell him that…

in Life… You never know what is going to happen next.

you can't plan life like a screenplay… I decided to put my screen-play writing and acting abilities to test.

On the scheduled date, right from morning, I was pacing up and down, psyching myself as an astrologer, I was a palmist *cum* face reader *cum* horoscope reader… what not… Make-up, Costumes, spectacles, intense and serious…. My look?… Somewhat mysterious… I remembered postures various astrologers adopt… and… ready with tape-recorder where I can secretly tape the conversation, since I was going to give my first live performance as an astrologer.

At 9.50 AM, I was alone and was waiting for both Anil and Amit to come... Bell rang... They had come 10 Minutes early... I *Shall make them sit... and wait... for good 10 Minutes... I am a Big and Important person... I thought... but could not act like one...*

Officer in me did not permit delays specially on my account!.

Our discussion started immediately... I insisted, I shall see you one by one.

Also, there was no need to verify who was Anil and who was Amit... It was obvious the senior one was Anil...

Between them, I shall meet Anil first... seniority in age must be respected... It took me about 15 Minutes to convince him he should join Insurance Business... may be a big loss-adjusting company.

then he will not have to look back after 2015, all his difficulties will vanish!... But... till then, hold your morale high... I proclaimed.

Anil was looking disappointed, curious, sometimes as if he was listening to a joke.

I ignored and kept on...

At 10.15 AM, I finished with Anil... now... Amit... the engineer...

If Anil's face was a galore of expressions, Amit was totally expressionless.

I told him to appear for Government exams like UPSC etc. and then be ready for a bright future... Big House, Status in society, happiness all round.

I remembered Sanskrit subhashitam (good thought) meaning... (Speak truth, speak what is sweet, but never speak truth that is not sweet!)

(Satyam Bruyat, Priyam Bruyat, Na Bruyat Satyam Apriyam…)

We should be careful in speaking the truth. The purpose should be good and the words used and the manner in which they are spoken are important. So the value of truthfulness is relative to a situation!

According to the Indian scriptures while living in the world of relativity, truth can be interpreted in many ways.

By 10.25, my narration was over… I was confident I had given new and proper directions… to both Amit and Anil.

More importantly, I had helped Mandeep, by offering predictions exactly as per his desire.

At the end of the meeting, both handed me an envelope… with my name.

"I don't charge money… for making predictions. It is a social service(How true?")

"No money, sir, actually only an invitation for dinner and some cultural programme…"

When?

"Next Sunday…"

"OK"…

10.30am… Anil and Amit were gone.

One by one, I was removing my costumes and make up… first the spectacles and then the gandh or tikka [15]on forehead… I was happy with myself…

This is perfect example of putting my acting talent(?) for social good.

---

[15]   Coloured KumKum

I was about to dial Mandeep's cell no to tell him everything had gone well… as per plan.

At that precise moment the doorbell rang!… At the door were two youngsters…

"Yes?"

"Sir, good morning. Do you Know Mr Nayyar? He sent us… We are his sons…

I am Anil and this is Amit…"

What? If you are Anil and Amit, who were they?

Who 'they', sir?

This was one time I was not required to act while stammering… "No… No… I mean… Yeah… Yeah… Leave it… Leave it… Just like that you see… Welcome… to both of you… Are you… little late or something?"

"Papa told us about your building behind HDFC Bank. we went there… and then realized Papa meant HSBC… and here we are… sorry for 30 minutes delay… We have heard a lot about you…"

Heard about me? What?

That you are an astrologer and this is your first tour to Mumbai.

I see… Good… What now?

I decided to repeat the whole show… (*Social service…*)

I made predictions… But I realized that I was gripped by something…

They say, "Practice makes one perfect!"

And, I was sure this was more emphatic performance than the earlier one…

Thank God but it was over in 20 Minutes…

What a relief? I was very tired and… satisfied…

If predictions come correct… Good…

If not, then I shall say "Life is the best teacher… It teaches everything." (Zindagi se seekho. Zindagi sub seekha deti hain)

(Life is the best teacher… It teaches everything)

I am OK either way…

Later in the evening

My evening was not OK at all… I was shocked when…

I realized that the first two boys were sent by a top executive in my client's office to sell tickets for a charity show… To be fair to my client, he had sounded me about it, which had slipped my mind… It turned out that they were event-sales-men and were trained to put up with *all the nonsense that I uttered in the hope of selling me tickets…*

They had no idea about Loss-adjuster and UPSC exams…

They were told to deliver tickets to me, whether or not I buy them… which they obeyed…

I did not buy tickets… But Luckily, I also did not charge them for my predictions(???).

More than One Year Later… (Nov 2013)

I met Mandeep in Mumbai and asked now rather shakily," How are your sons? What are they doing?" (We had not met in between…)

"They are doing good… They have come out of depression… thanks… Your predictions were correct… *but also, no thanks*'!"

Contrary to my expectations, It was Anil who had passed UPSC exams and was joining Government Department soon… and… It was Amit who had taken Loss-Adjuster's profession… He had passed necessary exams and was doing very well…

However, I am not happy with you…

Why did you alter what I had told you to say about Anil and Amit?

Whaaat? I was puzzled. I could not offer any immediate answer!.

Later, I checked up the sound-recording…

Only to realize what I had predicted was as follows…

I had told Anil to pass UPSC exams and Amit to be a Loss-Adjuster.

Predictions made by me by mistake… had come correct…

everything had happened as per predictions… by mistake!

I remembered… Something had gripped me…

I had spoken… but whose words? Was it destiny speaking herself? or was it just a coincidence?

How can I tell Mandeep it was not me… it was somebody else!…

Whole world knows Insurance losses can be adjusted… There are several expert Loss-Adjusters.

But can you adjust your predictions?… was the question before me.

Should I tell Mandeep the truth?… about what had actually happened when predicting. Will he believe me?

Like I told in the beginning, "Supernatural does not care whether you believe in it or not."

By the way, at least do you believe me?

If 'no', then no problem…

But, if your answer is 'yes'… Then I promise you one thing.

No more predictions from my side in this life.

Never shall I act as an astrologer… even by mistake!

Since I sincerely believe that… Life is the best teacher… It teaches everything. (*"Zindagi se seekho… Zindagi sub seekha deti hain…"*)

===

11

Ravi, Vaishali Teacher And Anti-D Gang & Mumbai Monorail

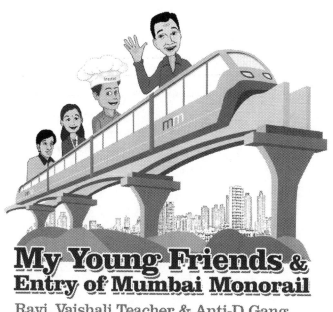

My Young Friends &
Entry of Mumbai Monorail

Ravi, Vaishali Teacher & Anti-D Gang

… AND THE HEART SANG 'TANG, TANG, TANG'

{"To hell with 'What will happen to the world or… or to this generation'?
I shall do my bit… whenever the opportunity comes… and that bit at that moment was… joining them in the dance!
Tang… Tang… Tang"}

Note from Vaishali Teacher to Ravi's parents read as under…

Please treat this matter as urgent.
    "Till you come and meet me, Ravi will not be allowed to sit in the class room"
    Sd-
    Vaishali Patil
    Class- Teacher
    Class VIII; Division B.

This meant that somebody had to go to school urgently. Since his parents were out of Mumbai, as a close friend, I was requested by them to visit the school.(They told me on phone: *Maybe you can say that you are the guardian or have an authority letter… nowadays they don't allow anyone to attend school. I shall send email to this effect.) I agreed!*

In the school, it was a cheerful morning atmosphere. The prayer of "Guru Brahma, Guru Vishnu(Teachers are Gods)" was being played… Atmosphere had become serene.

Prayer over, the classes began… I met class - teacher Vaishali (who taught my nephew Ravi)and I was surprised to find out that Ravi was not paying much attention to his home-work assignments.

Actually, I had a very high opinion about Ravi, since it appeared that Ravi had a very versatile personality. Not only did he have excellent culinary skills but he also excelled at doing small chores and purchases. He had a talent for getting competitive prices from 2-3 shops and ascertaining quality before effecting a purchase.

To me, this was very impressive! Ravi was a good candidate for becoming a hospitality professional, or Purchase Executive or even doing some business.

But for that he has to clear basic courses… like 10th standard, 12 th standard etc. and only then he can get admission to hospitality courses.

However, in the meeting with the class-teacher, there was not much use in sharing these special skills of Ravi, *when he does not do homework on time*! I shall ask him about this and sort out the matter but here I was wondering, how to conclude this discussion? I told the teacher about the movie 'Tare Zamin Par' (Stars on earth) and character of the teacher Nikumbh not forgetting to add that teachers should emulate him!… Teacher heard me, said nothing… *if I was in your place, I would emulate Nikumbh…* I had said… No response from the teacher!.

'These stars i.e. children should not get lost on the earth'... was the song from that movie haunting my mind.

In the movie *Taare Zamin Par*; *Ishaan Nandkishore Awasthi* is an eight-year-old boy who dislikes school and fails every exam! He finds *all subjects* <u>difficult</u>, He always becomes target of some teachers and classmates, solely for making fun. But Ishaan's private world is rich with wonders that he is unable to convey to others, magic of colour and animated animals. He is an artist whose talent is unnoticed so far.

For new teacher Ram Shankar Nikumbh, an instructor at the Tulips School for young children with <u>developmental disabilities</u>, it is a challenge!

He tells them he can provide extra tutoring that will help Ishaan, highlighting the boy's artistic ability evident in his many paintings and other creative works.

Nikumbh subsequently brings up the topic of dyslexia in class, and offers a <u>list of famous people who were dyslexic</u>.

In the climax of the film, Ishaan wins the school-competition by putting his painting skills to use.

Film ends approximately in two hours and forty five minutes. It is a screen-play which is compact and dramatic events are woven in a manner which take us to a happy climax and resolution of the problem.

I was very much impressed by Ram Shankar Nikumbh's character played by Aamir Khan. I was looking for an opportunity to emulate him. Here was a tailor - made opportunity! I decided to try technique of *motivation*. In near future, On Sunday, 2nd February 2014, Monorail in Mumbai was to commence its first trip and would run between 7am and 3pm. I promised Ravi and his other friends that if they complete their homework quickly on Saturday evening itself,

I shall take them on the *Monorail journey from Wadala to Chembur.*

Motivation theory seemed to have worked. Everybody had finished their homework… and as promised; Ravi along with his five friends were ready by 5 30am to go to Wadala Monorail station.

We reached Wadala Station at 6.30 am, hoping we will be among the first to reach there; but no!! There was a crowd of almost 1000 plus, already waiting there. With no other option, we too stood in the queue. It was a very enthusiastic crowd. Chants of *Ganapati bappa morya*[16] were in the air at regular intervals. Latest songs like '*Toone Mari Entry yaar, Dil mein Baji Ghanti yaar Tang*' (the moment you enter, my heart sings Tang) were being played on small tape recorders and people were making merry of this God sent opportunity! Sunday was a picnic day for them… and *Monorail* was to commence its first journey in India in Mumbai at Wadala!… History was being created, but the Police must have never expected this big gathering… Crowds like Ganapati festival to welcome *Monorail*! They were doing their best to control the situation! *Monorail* authorities announced that 1st train will leave soon. This was welcomed by '*Ganapati bappa moraya*'! The announcement continued… In place of tickets, some coin like thing was being issued as ticket. Again chants of *Ganapati Bappa*!… At the top of the queue was a gentleman, named Sunil, who was excited and waiting for his turn to enter the *Monorail*!

---

[16]   Popular group chant in Mumbai to commence any activity (in the name of Lord Ganesh)

Ravi and his friends had a brilliant idea... Why not interview him? With a mobile phone camera, we went there keeping one of of friends to hold our place in the queue.

On Sunil's face were expressions reading,"When will my number come?"

"It will come when it has to come" (Hindi Song-Aayega, Aayega Aanewala) was the only answer we could provide with expressions, gestures.

Interview began... ('I' is interviewer and 'S' is Sunil)

I: *Congratulations.*
S: Thanks.
I: *Your Name please?*
S: Sunil.
I: *How are you feeling today?*
S: On the top of the world!.
I: *Top of the World?*
S: I mean... Top of the queue!...
I: *How did you come here?*
S: I work at Andheri. I finished my 2nd shift by 12am... I took a train, to Dadar, then a bus and I reached here at 1 30am and formed the queue.
I: *What brought you here?*
S: Question on his face... no response.
I: *We mean what is your motivation?*
S: (Sunil organized his thoughts as under with lot of pauses)

Oh! I have done it for *Lalbaugcha Raja* (extremely popular Ganesh idol of Mumbai) and...

Navaratri Festival at Mahalaxmi also.

Being first in the queue... sometimes I succeed, sometimes I don't!

Whenever I have succeeded to be amongst top five, my next few weeks go well! I am on a high as if...

I have achieved something... I feel good... no... no.

I feel great!... My job is very routine and monotonous... 'capturing' this place in the Top 5 provides me with... change from routine and yes... some excitement...

Also, my children get impressed...

All of us congratulated him... It was a day of great achievement for Sunil... Interview could have gone on and on... but, the ticket counter opened... Sunil bought the coupon-coin, went up to the station... soon the train will come... and...

He will fly high... initially, for next few minutes in train and later on for next few weeks... *in his life*!

Here, I was getting a bit irritated by all this activity, noise and hoopla of the crowd!

Will this *Monorail* not run tomorrow? I was wondering! When I expressed my feelings to Railway clerk, he became philosophical. Anything else can be in short supply in India, but philosophy... never! As it is, he was overwhelmed by this great response to their venture!

Railway clerk answered in Hindi and as if in a trance, "It will... if tomorrow comes, surely it will!... But remember, Brother, *tomorrow is tomorrow, not today! Another day! 24 hours away*!... Some great saint has said... *Live in present moment*." Railway clerk shared his knowledge with me& then looking directly in my eyes asked, "You think all these people who have gathered here think that tomorrow *Monorail* won't run or something? *But they want to enjoy the thrill today! You think they are fools?*"

"No… I don't know… I mean I am not sure!"… I struggled with an answer and before station clerk could bombard me further with his brand of philosophy, I escaped!… In that supercharged atmosphere, people had only one thing in mind! To enjoy their picnic at the *Monorail* station, preferably ending with a journey… they can settle for nothing less than that!…

I expressed to my young friends, "*Will the sky fall if we sit in Monorail tomorrow?*"

My friends were sure," We don't care how much time it takes,… Sit in the *Monorail* we will… and today itself!… We will have break-fast only after *Monorail* tour! Just tea till then…

I had no option but to wait… *Small price to pay for emulating Nikumbh sir.*

We got our coupons by 10 30am, entered the station by 11am and boarded the train soon thereafter! Mumbai from *Monorail*… exciting stuff! 'Wadala to Chembur' journey was never so very exciting… Exciting, because of waiting for about 4 hours in the queue!… and finally achieving something… Great thrill! *Ganapati Bappa Moraya*…

After the journey, which included at least 10 more *Ganapati Bappa Morayas,* we had good break - fast of Idli-wada outside the station… Picnic was cheap!… Ticket Rs. 11 /- So family of 3-4 people could enjoy their day in Rs. 500- including conveyance etc. to and fro from their residence!… That explained huge crowd of middle-class people that had thronged the Mono rail stations… No sensible family person can miss such economical pleasures.

After the journey, we were returning to our residence… Ravi had developed great respect for Sunil and was telling me!… If for becoming *the first person to sit in Indian Monorail*

Sunil sir has taken so much trouble of losing his sleep, standing in the queue etc, it stands to reason that for becoming *Top Chef* which is my ambition, I must work hard and complete my routine syllabus with whatever effort that is required!... What was I hearing?

I pinched myself!

Success... finally! I had taken all the trouble, for hearing this... Have I actually brought one boy on the good track of his career? I was very pleased with myself!...

I decided to go to school next day itself and meet Vaishali teacher... Tomorrow onwards, Ravi won't bother you, in fact will bother no one!.

At least, for not doing homework!.

Next day, I had a few business calls to attend in the morning... I reached school... and was sitting across the table with the teacher... There were three other students who were also standing in the corner of the room.

I narrated my *Nikumbh - like* success story to her! However...

Compliments which I expected from the teacher, never came!... May be she is stingy with compliments and praise!... *What will happen if I take these compliments seriously? or... what if they go to my head and bloat my ego? Let it be!...* some people are like that!... but her gaze was on the three children standing in the corner... Like a movement of camera panning, I also looked at them as a reaction.

Vaishali teacher said, "Just as you got inspired by Nikumbh Sir and Ravi got inspired by well-known chefs Sanjeev Kapur and Tarla Dalal, these friends got inspired by Movie 'D-Day'... They got the news that 'Don" was seen near Alibaug... So, they formed Anti-D gang, stole some money

129

from parents, went to Alibaug to catch the 'Don'… Here their parents were scared… What happened to their precious sons? The last that were seen, in the course of the day, was in the school… so we got involved!… So many questions by Police, parents… *Did they mention where they were going? Who are their friends? Did they really go out of school? What does CCTV show?? Any hope… or…? Or what? Nobody dared to say!*

School staff was getting both angry with hundreds of callers and feeling sorry for the parents.

Are these the same three guys? I asked.

"Yes… They are… After they got news that 'Don' was seen at Alibaug… They searched several hotels in Alibaug… Struggled for a very long time… By night, when they had no trace of Don, and were still searching for Don in some remaining hotels, Alibaug police got suspicious! They caught hold of them, spoke to their parents in Mumbai on phone and packed them off to Mumbai…"

My mouth was wide open… Not knowing what to say! Vaishali teacher continued, "What will Nikumbh teacher say to this and what will *you* do to them?… and to so many others like them? Any motivational stuff?"

It was easy for me to advise her yesterday! *You should emulate Nikumbh sir!* Here in school, a full generation like Ishaan, with their own peculiar set of problems… Just one Nikumbh won't help!… Single heroic act of motivation won't do! Just won't do!

The pride in me of having shown the 'way' to Ravi was evaporating.

No trace of 'motivational stuff' now… This time my body - language and stance had changed!…

I could only say," I salute you teachers for tackling so many problems on day-do-day basis!… You are the real sculptors who are expected to carve out something good out of hundreds of… stones or… or… lumps of clay! "I reached home by 7 pm on Monday…

At home, Ravi and friends were in a different world altogether! They must have described the *Monorail experience adding a lot of* 'masala' to their classmates! Today, they had become heroes in the eyes of their respective classmates! They had downloaded *youtube* song from movie *Gunday* "Tune Mari Entry aur…" The moment I entered, they welcomed me… I was in 'Bharat' pose (pose of leading Hindi actor of yesteryears Manoj Kumar) with hand covering my face, as if, I was greatly troubled by some problem like, *"What to do with this generation?* How to bring them up and keep them on track? and so on…"

My young friends put on the song on their PC 'Dil mein baji ghanti yaar, tang… tang… tang' and started dancing… with full energy at their command! I waited for some time… Then… My brain was getting into *music gear* with legs responding to the beat… first slowly and with a very odd Bharat pose of hand covering my face and then… full blast! and with my hands in air, forgetting about my 'Bharat' pose.

"To hell with 'What will happen to the world or… or to this generation'? I shall do my bit… whenever the opportunity comes… and that bit at that moment was… joining them in the dance! "Tang… Tang… Tang"

===

131

Part 3

In School and College as a Student

INTRODUCTION

I met these characters in my school / college days. These stories happened in the 1970s.

Ganya Barve was a clever boy but due to bad company became a noted gangster on whose life a film was made.

I met Pradip as a Voodoo - man in College Election days. But was he a Voodoo man as some of my friends had branded him?...

I met Neerja in the bhang episode that rocked our college-hostel on one Holi-festival Day...

I met Leela on one of the result-days in 3 rd year of Engineering...

Some of you must have seen the Hindi movie Anand directed by Hrishikesh Mukherjee. This movie was released on March 18, 1971, not only did it introduce great characters like Anand (Rajesh Khanna), Babu Moshai (Amitabh Bachchan), Dr. Kulkarni (Ramesh Deo)and several others but it also had one wonderful character 'Muralilal', who never appears on screen, in the movie. Anand keeps looking for 'Muralilal' and the closest he comes to Muralilal is in the character of Isabhai (Johnny Walker) who proves to be his 'Guru' (one up on him) by pretending that in Anand, he has found his long-lost friend 'Jaychand'.

Suffice to say, these are my 'Murarilals and Jaychands,' whom I met and made friends with!

==

12

Ganya Barve

GANGSTER

{After throwing an 'excuse me for a minute' glance at me, he made the first phone call as if in a rage: "Reach Mulund (Mumbai suburb) by 4 PM." and put the phone down.

He then made another call," I am going to Vasai (place near Mumbai) for Next call... he said I am off to... Colaba... and then another one to say I am off to Alibaug. (Colaba is part of South Mumbai and Alibaug is a coastal town near Mumbai) Now all the team members were alert. What would Anil tell them?}

Sometime between 1963 to 1966

I was in High School.

My mother was a teacher in a municipal school, and she would bring the answer- papers home for corrections. Computers were still not on the horizon and online evaluations unheard of.

I was studying at King George High School(now known as Raja Shivaji Vidyalaya) We lived in a housing society called Sahakar Nagar, Wadala in Mumbai. It was predominantly a lower middle-class community and their children would attend the municipal school.

Correction of answer papers was an annual activity for my mother. I too had a role in that, viz., to see what my friends' scores were.

The moment a paper was checked and marks given... 41,... 33 (passing marks), 29, 21 (a few failing marks), and sometimes high scores of 50s,60s, even 70s, and-- in some rare instances… an 80, a 90, and even a perfect 100 in one instance.

The moment marks would be known and the result was a 'pass,' there would be celebratory dance! This routine stuck and made a lasting impression on my mind…

Not only in school but later also in my pre-engineering Jaihind college and further when at the engineering college, when in some semesters securing a pass mark itself was an achievement, I would emulate these old municipal school friends of mine and break into a dance. From amongst these friends(?), some very (in)famous characters were born. Ganya Barve was one of them, on whose life a movie would get released in later years.

Late 1970s

Mumbai was different then! The phenomenon of gang wars on the streets of Bombay were quite common. This was a totally new way for youth to express their frustration: the angry young men of organised crime were different from past generations of rebels.

I completed my engineering course in 1977. In the semesters leading to the final year, I used to celebrate even for securing just a passing mark, but then I became ambitious and raised my goal to score at least a first class before breaking into celebrations!

At around the same time as my new-found first-class ambitions, some of my municipal school- friends were fast earning a reputation as dreaded criminals and first-class outlaws. After doing some sporadic stints in other organisations, I joined Insurance Company. True to childhood values (impressions of childhood), I would go walking to Dadar station carrying a lunch box. I often went down memory lane to earlier years during my walk, thinking of textile mill- workers going to work with a tiffin-box in their hands. The permanent workers would enter the mill gate flashing their identity cards, but the temporary labour would wait in a queue, waiting for their identity to be acknowledged.

Sometimes they would be admitted in for work and many times it was a no!… Looking back, I feel, this is where the system failed to provide jobs for youth, resulting in rebellious and frustrated youngsters taking to crime.

One Such Day in the Late 1970s.

I was walking towards the train station. "Anil's Bar," which lies on the way, was then run by a municipal school friend of mine. By normal materialistic standards he had made it big. He complimented me, "Sudhir, I appreciate you a lot!. You became an engineer: we respect you for all the hard work. By the way, what do you do?" On hearing my reply the next logical question was: how much do you earn?

And I replied, with all additions of perks Rs2100/- per month.

This reply disturbed him and the other five friends who were with him. All of them were shocked that for just a meagre sum of… Rs2100 per month, I was slogging from 9am to 7pm daily.

Anil, the bar-owner was at his expressive best! "What? After struggling for a full month, you earn only Rupees 2100? (Implying, we make much bigger amounts in just half an hour!)

This loud expression left me embarrassed. Nobody so far had insulted me so brazenly, that too for my low salary…

I had no response to offer!My head went down in shame, embarrassment, whatever one might call it-- but I was hit where it hurts most. I even felt tears in my eyes.

Now the twist of destiny was yet to come.

At the same instance, the hotel-phone rang. One needed to be privileged, so to speak, to own a telephone connection in those days. I (I got my first telephone connection only on January 21, 1985, after being in queue for a few years! I can forget my birth-day but not the day I got a phone connection)

Anil answered the phone, and what he heard from the other side must have been hard to digest for him, as he looked visibly uncomfortable.

He hung up and was thinking hard. After throwing an *'excuse me for a minute'* glance at me, he made the first phone call as if in a rage: "Reach Mulund (Mumbai suburb) by 4 PM." and put the phone down.

He then made another call," I am going to Vasai (place near Mumbai) for some urgent matter ".

Next call… he said I am off to… Colaba… and then another one to say I am off to Alibaug.(Colaba is part of South Mumbai and Alibaug is a coastal town near Mumbai)

Now all the team members were alert. What would Anil tell them?

Anil ordered," In separate vehicles, and by Agra Road all of us shall reach Vikhroli. Let's see what happens tomorrow!)

All of them got up… they were in a hurry now… I could imagine what kind of phone call that must have been!

Anil was now nervous… he turned his attention to me… "Sudhir, sorry yaar… We are in a hurry… shall meet you at leisure!"

Inside I was fuming,… thinking about how to retaliate. How should I respond to the "below the belt" hit that he had delivered on me, some minutes ago. I was gathering myself… maybe I could have just let it pass… but frankly I was unable to come to terms with that comment, "Only 2100 Rupees?" I was seething with anger.

He might have met me at leisure (aaram se)a month later… 6 months later or never at all: I had to respond today, quickly—it was now or never!

"If you can convey the right message at the right time, it creates the best impact!" Courtesy _ Movie *Trishul*)

I said, "When I go to Matunga, I am never required to say that I am going to Vikhroli. I do what I say and go to Matunga.

I don't have to make up stories… Whenever I go to any place, I openly say I am going there and actually do it!

This was the most aggressive response I could think of.

My response could have been anything but all that I could think of then was this one!

Anil did not know what to say… He tapped on my shoulder trying to convey "I quite understand what you want to say."

Anil and his team rushed to their car… Last to leave was Ganya Barve, in a white shirt and blue jeans with a well built, muscular body. This was one character who would score marks in 70s, 80s, and even 90s… He used to be delighted when he heard his scores and would break into a dance. I clearly felt he was distinctly different from the stereotypical gangster…

A movie was later made on Ganya Barve's life(Shoot out at some place!)That movie makes me believe that here was a guy who walked the 'decent-man-path' for the longest but finally succumbed and joined the 'wrong company' when he could not get a decent job. Unfortunately, he was later even falsely implicated in a crime because of the *company* he kept.

He was the last guy to board Anil's vehicle. Just while boarding, he paused and said to me... "*What you say has a lot of substance.*"(Tumhare baat mein bahut dum hain, Boss)

All of them kept travelling on their chosen paths...

In 2009

'They' went their way and I mine!

Most of them are no more—killed... dead in police - encounters!

As for me, I can still do what I say!

My son passed his engineering and went on to join one of the IIMs (Indian Institute of Management)... In a rare instance, when my son asked me if I had to give him one piece of advice, what would it be?, I said: "If you can do what you say and go wherever you want to without fear of the consequences, then I think you should consider yourself successful!... Never try to measure your success in terms of the money you make... the means always has the most prime place!

When I narrate this story to youngsters, they refuse to believe it!

They keep on saying it is a figment of my imagination!

It would take them still some more time to understand that sometimes '*facts are stranger than fiction.*'

===

13

Dilipbhai and Sarita Shetty

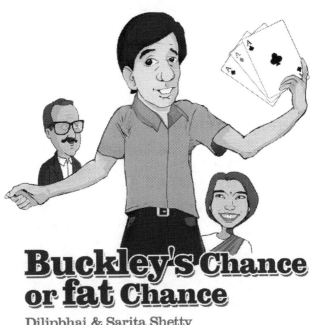

Buckley's Chance or fat Chance

Dilipbhai & Sarita Shetty

BUCKLEY'S CHANCE

{Looking at my posture and predicament, one girl, co-traveler in the bus Sarita Shetty came to me and whispered to me: Do you have good cards? If so, don't worry, our group shall loan you the amount...

They must have been rich people... offered me a whole 100 rupees as 'Risk Capital' and with the condition "We expect 10% return on our investment."... If it is OK with you, *Play... Play as long as you must, as hard as you can*!...}

T his story is dedicated to the VJTI 1977 batch's direct/indirect participants such as:

Nittin Keni
Naren Desai
Nagesh Hanagodu
Vilas Mhatre(for rejuvenating the Buckley's/Fat/Minimum Chance concept)
Harsh Karande(for finding the concept interesting)
The Mumbai University tour group to FTII, Pune.

Background

All of us keep getting chances in our lives.
Some of us make good use of these and some of us do not.
There are some chances which one would classify as 'slim to nil' chances.

For instance, my friend Harsh has mentioned two incidents in the 'slim to nil' category: 1) trying to put the oozed out toothpaste back into the tube or 2) win the Mega Lottery/Lotto (odds of 1 in 243 Million or some such astronomical number)

Both have a Buckley's chance of success!

Note on Buckley and Buckley's chance
William Buckley:

William Buckley was an English Convict who escaped from the prison in Australia in 1803.

You may know that Australia was originally a penal colony of England. Mr Buckley decided to elope and thought that he can walk along the coast and reach Sydney - several hundred miles away.

After a few weeks, Buckley was in bad shape with hunger. While walking through Lorne area, he saw a stick stuck in the ground and decided to use it as a walking stick.

As he was walking, the native aboriginal people saw him. The stick he took was the stick used in the burial of the dead aboriginal people. To Mr. Buckley's great luck, the aboriginal people thought he was the spirit of their ancestors and took great care of him. Buckley became part of them.

After some 30 odd years, some English saw him within the aboriginal village and were amazed that he survived 30 years with them.

But in spite of his luck in using the stick, Mr. Buckley never reached Sydney.

The popular Australian idiom, "Buckley's Chance" implies that there is a very little probability of success –Like "Fat Chance" phrase in US, it means minimum chance)

In addition to above two possibilities, there could be other possibilities also.

Read this one, and tell me, if it qualifies as 'Buckley's' chance.

Year: 1976, Month: December
Location: Room No. 301, D Block,
C.O.E. (College of Engineering) Hostels

My room-partner Mihir came with exciting news: The following week, both of us had been selected to go to FTII, the Film and Television Institute of India on an all expenses paid trip. Mihir and I had made it to the final list of 50 people (our 3rd room-partner, Mahesh, was the silent/ studious type and definitely not much interested in filmy activities.) We were going as part of a Mumbai University students group to FTII Pune for two days and a night

Some ATKT(carry over) exams were nearing. Fortunately, there was just one paper… Geology.

After that, was the Big Final Year Exam.

The following year, hopefully, I would have graduated with an Engineering degree. It was just a matter of time.

The Following Week… 7 AM Monday.

Since it was a University sponsored trip for cultural exchange, a bus full of boys and girls departed from the University Club House, Churchgate.

Early in the morning with lots of songs… *In the morning… by the sea.*

If I were a little girl and if I were to marry…

Most of the participants were from schools where the medium of instruction was English, it appeared…

(Trips with kids instructed in Marathi never had such crafted songs, so I stuck to songs like: 1) Karacha kay tula karacha kay" (Marathi folk-song) or "Dekha na hai re socha na" from the movie *Bombay to Goa*.

Same Afternoon

Visit to FTII was quite interesting… Shooting Floors… Library, Canteen, Banyan Tree…

One student was busy reciting a dramatic hindi passage meaning, "I have committed a sin; neither my father knows about it, nor my mother."

The passage was quite long… 2 pages… He was struggling with the lines…

We prompted him, acted as proxy and cheered him, thinking, "One day he will become an important actor."

He was Dilipbhai, and he liked to call himself a struggler… He used this 'Minimum Chance' term that time.

"Becoming a star in this world is a *minimum chance*. Actor I am and can become a better one… not a star!".

I did not understand what he was talking about but could gather that becoming a star must be very difficult.

(**Dilipbhai,** film and television actor, in Mumbai, died of a heart attack in 2000, best known for his roles in television serials.)

Until then, I was of the opinion that 4 years of study after 12thgrade in school makes one an Engineer and 3 years at FTII after 12 th grade makes one an Actor! Little was I to know that it requires a whole life-time to really qualify as an

Engineer, an Actor, in fact any profession for that matter… In 3-4 years, one can only get a Degree/ Diploma and a certificate to practice the profession.

FTII, that time had several learned Professors for Film-analysis, and while analyzing a movie, one of them must have used this term, *'minimum chance'*…

Staying arrangements were good at Amir Hotel, Pune.

Evening Chhayageet (famous TV program with movie songs in those days) was not to be missed.

No place to have camp-fire… so our performances of singing, mimicry remained indoors.

Next Evening:

Some movie at FTII, a visit to National Film Archives and the return journey began… From Pune to Mumbai late in the evening…

We halted at Lonavala…

There was no expressway then, so driving in the night was not recommended… and most importantly, there was still some unused money from the budget.

"We shall sleep here (pointing to one hotel)" Ramesh Mhatre from T.E. Mech, Sardar Patel College of Engineering our Group-leader announced.

Nobody could sleep… Then began a game of Flush… (Teen patti). We (Mihir and myself) had a decent amount of Rs. 25/- left with each of us. We decided to keep Rs. 5/- and put everything else on the bets as our 'middle-class' decision of playing safe!

I was quick to 'pack-up' in the earlier games… The kind of cards were never good.

This strategy worked and I lasted until the last two games, with a total of Rs 11/- still with me.

As per the convention, the second last game was of 4 cards not 3. There, I 'packed up' in the 1st round itself.

Again no luck… Now all I had was Rs. 10.50/-

I wanted to win at least one game and here I was, having survived until the last game, in spite of one loss after another.

The last game of the night was of two cards. Cards were distributed…

After round 1, 15 players had remained in the field, with a series of 'pack-ups.' I had decided to fight until the end…

I was playing 'blind.'

I had heard, *"The game is not over, until it is actually over"*…

Also there were two incidents in the flash-back of my life, which were encouraging me to play till the end…

Flashback 1: Sometime in October 1975

Mihir and I joined a game of cards on the road-side… A typical trickster gang… 3 cards… 1 queen… The performer would shuffle the cards in a such a manner that you could never identify where the queen is. Of course, that was also the game: Where is the queen?

We were watching from a little distance.

Mihir thought he had understood it and cracked the code.

Trickster gang won't allow us to simply watch the game from a distance… either you play or quit the scene… don't just be an observer.

We took the bet: Mihir looked so sure…

He tried 11-12 times to locate the queen, but every time he was wrong.

1 Rupee per bet twelve times… Rs.12 gone… No money left now!

But can *would-be engineers* quit as losers? That too from a trickster gang?

I came forward… Now I thought, I had cracked the code. I said to the performer: Let me play this last game but I have no money. He allowed… and… and… Lo and Behold!

I could locate the queen, but without the stakes, there was no reward.

(Did the road-side trickster allow me to win, as there was nothing at stake anyway? But this is not the question that you ask yourself at such times…)

With our punctured ego now slowly recovering, we came back to the hostel…

Flashback 2: Year 1976

In the Hydraulics Oral exam, the last two students to be examined were Mangesh and I.

It was about 7 PM, and the examiner was tired--. so were we!.

Examiner decided to take our oral exam together… not one-by-one.

One question for Mangesh, one for me. We were answering in that dark Hydraulics lab. There was one last question he put to both of us: Value=2 marks.

I gave one answer and Mangesh another. The examiner asked: does one of you want to change the answer, because one answer is right and another is wrong. I had great temptation to change my answer, thinking: "Surely, Mangesh can't be wrong." As for Mangesh, he was supremely confident about his answer.

Both of us stuck to our answers… Miracle was that, I was right and Mangesh was wrong! I got 2 marks more than him in that oral exam. From that day, I was convinced that anything in the last round is lucky and good for me.

It seemed "*I normally reserve my best for the last*"

I remembered both these incidents in flashback mode but **Tonight… and here… in this game of cards,** what is in store for me? The series of ATKTs was quite bad, and it had to end this time. I won't ask money from my parents this time… I shall have to earn it… here and now… in this game…

And I was playing blind, firstly because of the '*Last Game Lucky*' theory, and secondly because playing blind was cheaper.

After you have seen the cards, you have to bet double the amount spent by 'blind'… Not 50 Paise but 1 whole Rupee…

But, I belonged to middle-class and, like it or not, 50 paise also had its value, so why lose it playing 'seen'?

If they are 'so-so' type cards, I thought I would ask for a 'Show' and end the story.

After a few rounds, I saw my cards…

Wonder of wonders…

It was 2 aces. I now can't remember which, but it was 1 red and 1 black. I continued with 1 Rupee now…

After 7 rounds, there were the final 2 players in the ring… one boy from National College and me…

If I remember right, his name was Shetty… He had seen his cards and I mine…

Most unexpected player like me playing raised so many eyebrows! All the 25-30 players (who had now' packed up' for the night) gathered around us, cheering both of us...

Opponent Shetty had his backers and supporters, not only in cheering him but even financially.

Round 11: I had my last rupee left: who will finance me? Where is Mihir in this crowd?

Nowhere to be seen.

Unexpected situations make unlikely people... your friends.

Another Shetty in the group came to me... A girl, Sarita Shetty... and her two class-mates. Were they from Ruia College? Not very sure...

No shortage of cheer-leaders for me, but in a game like this...

Honey, it's all about money! For me, there was neither honey nor money...

I never said it with words, but my whole body-language must have been speaking, even shouting that sooner rather than later, I was going broke...

From my side, I was also engrossed in different worries... What if my opponent also had 2 aces?

In that case, one who asks "Show" first, is the loser...

So no way I am going to ask for "show".

I shall play whole night or even on the next day... and so on...

What was happening in 'his' mind? And where is the money to keep playing?

Looking at my posture and predicament, one girl, co-traveller in the bus.

Sarita Shetty came to me and whispered to me: Do you have good cards? If so, don't worry, our group shall loan you the amount...

They must have been rich people... offered me a whole 100 rupees as 'Risk Capital' and with the condition "We expect 10% return on our investment."... If it is OK with you, *Play... Play as long as you must, as hard as you can.*

Inspiring words...

Even if the game goes to Rs. 5/- per round...

I can now 'outlast him'...

More such loans followed... The total amount went up to Rs. 1000/- plus. I was thinking, would this lead to into hundreds of thousand rupees?

(Millions of Rupees was unthinkable those days. Marathi movie was possible in less than half a million rupees)...)

This was my 'Minimum' or 'Buckley's' chance to become a lakhpati... (1 lakh is 100,000)

Dilipbhai had said it was like *minimum chance* to become a big star...

For me, it was a reality... could my dream come true?

Will it mean no need to complete engineering and work for life?

But dreams don't last long. It had to be over sooner than later... albeit on a positive note.

Opponent Shetty must have realized that he was up against an unexpected opponent but with strong cards. He asked for a show... He had '2 Nines'.

1 black, 1 red... He was confident...

I was more than confident...

Actually, I had trouble keeping a cool face.

I was feeling like dancing with joy but I had watched some movies of Clint Eastwood and Charles Bronson…

After the job is done, they walk away coolly… One more job… just a jaaa… b… (I really like American pronunciation… jaaa… b)

All expenses deducted… I won Rs. 1000/- plus…

I could finance all my ATKTs if these happen in future…

Exam fees was Rs. 80 /- I think, or was it Rs. 40/-? No problem…

The only thing I remember now is that, I could not walk away with the treasure… coolly… All the guys, even the girls, asked for a party.

(Where do Clint Eastwood, Charles Bronson and the likes go after they have done a jaa… b?) with all the treasure(some guys called it 'loot') in my pocket I went to celebrate with the entire group… to a small tea-stall at Lonavala ST Bus Depot. They expected me to throw a party as per the custom.

Tea for all in that cold night… Never had it tasted better…

Some guys even ate pav-bhaji (a famous dish from Mumbai… spicy vegetable with local bread), I came back to Mumbai with Rs.700 plus. One more thing: both the Shettys (my opponent and my financier) offered to share the expenses of the party: after hearing my story of planning to fund my arrears examination (A.T.K.T.) fees, they were moved to tears.

Was it the biting Lonavala cold that made them have tears in their eyes?

These are doubts which are creeping in now, not then)

At VJTI Office after I came back...

When I went to pay the exam fees... Menon, the administrator) informed me that the fees were already paid... Ah... by whom?

It was my father... who else?

So my ATKT was not a closely guarded secret as I had imagined.

Also my great plan of financing my future ATKTs with this money did not materialize, because... after that, I never had any ATKT...

I became an engineer along with VJTI1977 batch... as per schedule... after some initial struggle but in the end with First-Class.

That money in the wallet remained with me for a very long time...

After about 8-10 years... the wallet disappeared. It has not yet been found!

Nobody stole it for sure... it must be somewhere...

If I had bought some shares like Reliance, Colgate then I would have become a millionaire just on that...

There is only a rare chance, that I will find it...

Can you call that Buckley's chance?

Post Script

1) Dilipbhai was right: he became a well-known actor, but not a big star.
2) I passed B.E. Final exam in 1977 and until today, I have been working as Engineer since the past several years.

Must be because, those exams were passed on my father's hard-earned money and *not on the loot...*

Also.

It appears all our fathers kept saying something *profound...*

One of my friends Murali mentioned about his father telling him to give even if it is *'Yath-kinn-chith' (very small)*

My father used to talk about money earned after sweating or hard-earned money ('paseene ki kamai')... I joked about it then.

What has sweat (paseena) got to do with money?

Today, I know...

===

14

Voodoo Pradip

160

IT IS ELECTION -TIME!!

{Paddy kept repeating, "Just confess once, that you have used the black-magic man to defeat me. I don't mind losing... but how could you fall that low?" (*Knife was twisted in with precision*}

In May 2014, national elections got over, but there are State Elections, Municipal Elections happening all the while... at one place or the other...

And every time elections are announced, and Election Times... are near, I keep remembering my college-days in late 1970s...

Not that anything much different happens in elections anyway. It is like the drama *Mouse Trap* performed for generations by different cast and crew. *Actors may change... Drama remains the same.*

The end result is never good in such bitterly fought battles... Battles get over, but scars and injuries remain!

During the college days you keep thinking you are in a very big world and events such as these elections appear to be life-size at certain points... But today, after a big gap of 40 years, you realize the futility of getting worked-up at the smallest of provocations. It could have escalated into a physical brawl any time...

Realizing all this, college elections were discontinued after 2005.

Now-a-days, it is just nomination of the students by professors to such posts. and they get selected through interviews.

However, in my view, getting selected is different from getting elected. In one of the Alumni meets, I met one such 'appointed' Secretary to the post, and he was happy about it... But the excitement and fun of election times is totally different.

Time: Late seventies. C.O.E.
(College of Engineering, Mumbai)
Election Time

Second year of Engineering year was considered a good time to contest elections but the third year is considered the best bet. By the final year ofthe degree course... priorities are different. Good grades, placements: these thoughts occupy your mind.

Usually, the Irani restaurant near our Hostel would down the shutters at 12 midnight and we never missed having our last cup of tea... Mihir, Mahesh and I.

When we were in the third year, a meeting happened in our room at 12.15 am after we had finished our midnight tea session.

Mihir was very keen to contest the elections. He was an astute politician too.

We had taken samples of student opinions and since he came across as an aggressive personality, people expressed reservations on the issue of voting for him.... A great new strategy was cooked! I was at that time struggling with some subjects and therefore was ruled out for contesting the elections. Too risky we felt, considering that our plan was to pass Engineering in precisely four years. So the best option was Mahesh, a quiet, studious type and a complete surprise package... Mihir would lead with campaign process.

Against Mahesh was a guy Paddy from my Branch(Civil Engineering) and both Mahesh and Mihir were from Mechanical. Paddy was a scheming kind of a fellow.

Something about Paddy here…

He came in the second year into our college after passing first year in some college at Sangli or Karad. He had taken some three years to pass the first year of engineering because he had called his professor as 'Kauva (meaning crow)', which was his code-name amongst students. When the professor noticed it… Remember, It is never good to make fun of a Professor, who is known for his vengeful ways.

No great astrologer was required to predict what would happen to Paddy… After a struggle of three years, he could pass 1st year and landed in our College under the scheme of transfer of University.

One more thing I noticed that even as a student, he always carried a brief-case. No other student I remember, had this habit…

In the Run-up to the Elections:

Mihir did a very aggressive campaign. [*I really wonder, what happened thereafter but he never entered Indian politics.*

Some early promises are fulfilled and some are not…]

Paddy countered Mihir wit for wit but public speaking skills of Mihir were far superior to those of Paddy. However, as regards, networking or one on one communication, Paddy had natural talent plus he was rich and did not mind spending money on such activities.

Paddy was particularly angry with me, because he used to say openly referring to me, "Why should he campaign for rival Mechanical group Mahesh? Which loyalties are bigger? Room-partner or branch - mate?"

According to him, branch loyalty was more important. I did not agree.

Paddy was afraid, I shall switch some Civil Engineering votes for the Mechanical branch candidate Mahesh. This was gaddari(disloyalty) with my Branch. Room-partner loyalty apart, it was impossible for me to like him, because of his scheming personality who would bring politics into everything. (Where is he? Again, he is nowhere to be found today...)

There were 13 important posts for which elections were to be conducted. Posts like Gen. Secretary (Social), EDSA (Engg. Degree Students' association) secretary, gymkhana secretary... There was a little noticed post mentioned at the bottom of notice U.R. (University Representative) Only 2 candidates applied for the post, since it was advertised for the 1st time. Rakesh was the only other man apart from Mihir to have applied for that post. He withdrew after meeting with Mihir. What must have happened in that meeting only the two of them know! It could be anything of *Saam, Daam, Dandh or Bhed.* (use of Negotiation, Money, Punishment and 'divide and rule' in that order)

I don't know how, but it was Paddy who won the election by just two votes. There was gossip: Some bogus voting, tampering with vote-boxes had happened... But on the face of it, we went and met Paddy to congratulate him... He said," Today is my day, I expect your co-operation in running the affairs".

We said "sure"... All very prim and proper.

One year passed by… All the activities happened on schedule… But… nobody forgot the bitterness which had crept in during the elections.

Time: The following year… again… Election Time:

Paddy and Mihir both had become more ambitious now… They had formed their panels again… As per convention, nobody from our batch was fighting election now, so they had to form panel from second and third year students.

Like they say, "*The idea of election is much more interesting than the election itself… The act of voting in itself is a defining moment.*"

Again candidates were chosen and battle-lines were drawn.

People were forced and locked into rooms, allowed to come out only after form-filling time was over!

Paddy had his own problems in whole of third year… Confident he always was! Now he became overconfident. This subtle change from confidence to overconfidence could not be noticed by himself but quite easily by any third person. Everybody noticed it except himself. Also, he opposed a tour planned by the department. So even our own branch-mates went against him. Besides, he was never popular with the faculty.

There were some faults with Mihir also, but… he was opposition… not ruling party. Ruling party cannot have defects. Anti-incumbency comes into play immediately.

In retrospect, Paddy's back was to the wall, what remained was twisting- in of the knife!…

Deadlines like," I want your answer in 15 Minutes" were given on a regular basis, warnings/ threats were issued frequently for example "You withdraw your candidate X, otherwise"…

Mahesh and I were in it but more as viewers or advisors…

This time apart from usual campaigning, Mihir did something extra… To bring a voo-doo specialist (or so the gossip said)… Pradip.

Voo Doo[17] Specialist Pradip

This was a totally different experience for all of us…

He was introduced as Face-reader to us…

To begin with, he assured Mihir and all of us that yes… *Victory will be ours*! He had some noticeable sign on his left foot… on asking him what it was, he replied that this is the punishment for all the black acts he does…

Fortune-telling: Session 1

Mihir requested Pradip to have a session of face-reading with us…

So, there actually happened a session of fortune– telling in our room… So many neighbours had assembled! Pradip was telling, "He will become this and he will become that." About Mihir, he said, he will remain amongst the top in his profession. But the googly[18] was when my time came to sit in front of him. He concentrated hard… and said, "Nothing. Nothing bad about him."

---

17   Black magic

18   In game of cricket, a trick-ball

Mihir was hopeful he will predict something great for me. As a special request, Mihir requested him to concentrate again on me. Same result! All that Pradip said was: "You are scared of something… what? He could not identify. Neither could I… Maybe scoring 1st Class marks was a tremendous pressure and the same was telling on me.

Fortune-Telling: Session2

This game was not to stop here. Mihir brought Voo-Doo Pradip's boss… somebody called Dhanesh.

He also assured Mihir, "Excellent results in Elections." Again for me, he had something good to say. He said, "OK, but it will take quite some time for him to come into his own."

Was it a genuine fortune-telling or just a front to hide their black-magic activities? Personally, neither Mahesh nor I found any black-magic vidhis(Black-magic rituals)… *Gossip said pooja was performed in a dark corner in Hostel… just after 12 am one night…*

Elections were conducted and it was now time for…

Election Results…

We were watching a movie *Mehbooba* (Rajesh Khanna, Hema Malini)at Chitra Theatre, when Mihir who went out of theatre in the interval, did not come back even after 20 Minutes after the movie began. We were wondering, where is he? He came after 30 Minutes or so in an elevated mood. All the seats for our panel… Clean sweep…

There was just one catch! One panel member was common to both the panels, and he won with maximum vote-margin. This was the only consolation prize for Paddy.

This time it was a reverse of the last year scene. It was Paddy who came to our room. He was quite drunk, and he congratulated us but did not forget to ask us," Did you use a black magic fellow to win elections?"

Mihir assured him," No such thing… we won on merit and good campaign… How can you even think like this? As a last punch, Mihir said, "Take it sportingly. You win some and lose some. Now we expect co-operation from you in running the affairs."

Paddy kept repeating, "Just confess once, that you have used the black - magic man to defeat me. I don't mind losing… but how could you fall that low?" (*Knife was twisted in with precision*)

Mihir answered, "Rumours! Just rumours! Knowing Paddy's weakness to understand high-sounding philosophy, I elaborated," This rumour is nothing but "an unverified account or explanation of events which is being circulated intentionally." I continued.

"'Truth' is always 'only one' and hence static; but 'rumour' can wear costumes of different colours, shapes… and forms: hence, it is dynamic and interesting."

I had a great example before me from Mahabharata when Yudhishthir said, "*Naro Va Kunjaro Va*! Someone called Ashwatthama was killed? (and then very softly)Man or Elephant, I don't know…

Some face-reader had come in the hostel, but are face-readers black-magic performers? God knows… Neither me nor Mahesh… not even Mihir."

============*====================*=============

15

Don Bhangwale

THE BHANG EPISODE

Rector: (Looking at 3 of us) Amitabh what? and taking
　　notes) Which branch? What is his surname?

3 of us: Hmmmm… No idea, sir.

Rector: We want to fix responsibility… Who is his best
　　friend?

1 of us: Hmm…

Finally I replied: I think Rajesh… (I did not say
　　Khanna) what if he had heard about Rajesh
　　Khanna?

So… no risk.

Rector: Which branch?
　　　　(It was difficult to place Amitabh and Rajesh in an
　　　　Engineering Branch…)

1978/79, 2-3 days after Holi (Indian festival to celebrate
Goddess Holikadevi's victory over evil…)

Location: Interrogation/Enquiry Room of Hostel
(Actually used as a store room to store table tennis
rackets, balls, cricket apparatus now converted into
Enquiry Room or simply E-Room)

Rector Samant (age 52) was a very serious man, and
was engaged in interrogating some 7-8 of us about the
Bhang Incident.

(About 55 students had brought a bhangwallah[19] to the Hostel, made thandai-bhang[20]and drank it! Result was bad… Most of the students were 'high' like a kite and could not even have lunch. Up to late night they were vomiting, dancing, laughing loudly… A Doctor was called, and parents of students who were in a serious condition were informed. As a result, a detailed enquiry was ordered which was in progress)

The only good part about him was his college-going daughter Neerja. At least 200 students waiting for one glance from her. I used to imagine she once actually smiled at me.

But here in the E-Room, the person we were dealing with was the glum-faced rector.

Enquiry in Progress: Part 1

Rector: Are you aware how much loss happened because of what students did after having bhang?

2 Tables, 3 doors, 6 Chairs, some water-glasses and window-panes were broken.

Entire list is here… Are you aware what is the total damage?

All of us: No Sir.

Rector: Rs. 10, 325 /-. Who is responsible?

(This was an Engineering College, so to assess the damage which normally would take a fortnight or even a month in an Arts or Commerce college, this was done in a day's time. Tough luck!)…

---

[19]   Expert cook who makes Bhang (intoxicating liquid, ingredients mentioned in the story)

[20]   Colloquial for Bhang

All of us: Sorry Sir. (We thought 'sorry' will suffice.)

Rector: College will not bear this, all of you will! and Shinde what were you saying? *Rotally Tolright…*

(Instead of Totally Alright?)

And you Bhagat, what were you asking Subramanium? *"Why are you putting your bhang into my bhang?* Aren't you ashamed? (We were ashamed,… but past was past… Why can't Samant Sir live in present moment? We were not sotally Rober but Totally Sober today…).* You will make good all the damages… ok?

All Of us: Yes Sir and Very sorry sir(actually *Thank you sir*, Total of 55 students drank bhang, so per person it was coming to approx. Rs. 190/- per person.(Add Rs. 125 /- share of Bhang) Not bad… We were wondering, after all this violence and breakage, this much damage was quite OK. I mean 55 of us went intoxicated and went berserk after having bhang thandai prepared by <u>Ram Sharan Don Pandit Bhangwale</u>[21]… I am sure most of the students went to their rooms and slept, may be vomited, but not indulged into violence.… only some breakages)

On Holi Day in COE (College of Engineering) Campus.

Today was Holi and we were denied permission from the Rector to celebrate HOLI in our Hostel campus. So *Pooja* was performed a little distance away in Class IV Staff -Quarters, fire was lit and we shouted in the names of all the rivals/

---

[21] Name of Bhang-expert. The longer the name, the more expert he is.

enemies / villains. There were two strong groups in the hostels. Everything about them was different. Their loyalty to Mess and how to run it, their election candidates… They agreed on one thing though… Tomorrow we should celebrate *Dhulwad*[22] day with… bhang [23]and thandai.

Have you seen the Hindi Movie *Don* starring Amitabh Bachchan?[24]

Yes, the same one which had dialogues like "Don is wanted in eleven countries, but to catch Don is not just difficult, it is impossible!" Amitabh would deliver such razor-sharp lines to the loud clapping by the audience.

In our College days, we were greatly impressed by that movie and more specifically by the bhang Song…

"Khai ke Paan Banaras wala… Khul jaye band akal ka taala".

(Once I eat Beetle Nut Leaf from Benaras city, my inactive brain becomes active)

Bhang with thandai needs preparation by an expert… *How and where to find him*?

No *google* or any search engine was available those days and no *Just Dial too either*… so it had to be word of mouth… and general knowledge.

We also did not have knowledge of the two bid system at that time… so no technical and price bids for a bhang – maker were invited. What we knew, however, was to identify a good bhang – maker for tomorrow and start only at 7pm on the night before, the night was going to be very difficult.

---

[22]   Next day of Festival holi
[23]   Intoxicating substance
[24]   Very famous Indian superstar

In such a situation, teams went all over Mumbai cityand finally one bhang-maker was identified.

His special qualification was that *he had made bhang for that song of Amitabh Bachchan*, 'Khaike Pan Banaras- walla' in *Don*, and he was assistant for bhang making in the song *'Jay Jay Shiv Shankar'*[25] from Movie *Aap ki Kasam*(with Rajesh Khanna)…

He even had a split second appearance in the movie *DON*… (He said, "I did a small role.")

By about 12.30 am, after lot of analysis, a deal was struck. Charges Rs. 375 /- plus conveyance Rs. 25/-. Total Rs. 400 /- List of materials required as per the slip (Actually, written on the reverse side of two bus tickets)…

Water
Sugar
Milk
Almonds
Watermelon/Cantaloupe seeds (dried and skinned)
Poppy seeds (khus khus)
Aniseed
Cardamom powder
Peppercorns (whole) (sabut kali mirch)
cannabis (bhaang) (Ram Sharan will bring)
Dried or fresh rose petals

We realized it's not our domain and paid him some additional money to bring most of the material except water, Milk and sugar.

---

[25]   Victory to Lord Shiva – A song

My friends were busy giving the impression that we were seasoned bhang – drinkers and needed something special this time.

On enquiry as to what kind of bhang we preferred:
The answer was classic…
Two types of bhang we don't want.

1)   One which intoxicates very fast
2)   One which intoxicates very slowly

Apart from these two, anything else will do…

Dhulwad Day: Day after Holi

With the specifications mentioned above, we had no means to know what *Ram Sharan 'Don' Pandit Bhangwale* made of it, but the next day he was there with his team at 9 AM and was on the job…

Someone had a brilliant idea… Let's not have breakfast… so that after we have thandai-bhang, we will really go very high… and then we can have food…

Our age was such that you tend to do all sorts of adventures…

Everybody followed this rule of no breakfast, only thandai and bhang.

After that sumptuous lunch was prepared… Only problem was that very few people could eat… Everybody was in seventh heaven… and flying… in different territories.

Some were dancing throughout…

Some were singing and laughing and looked like they will continue till the end * of the world.(*at least until the course ended)

Some started crying for the silliest of the reasons, like their hands were stuck in the trouser pockets and they could not take those out…

One boy, Dinesh Patti, was having bath, about 20 times in 2 hours after which he fell on floor because of fatigue.

Doctor was called… He examined all… and declared, "Most of them would be OK by tomorrow morning…"

When he visited my room, I was having hallucinations about my mother not giving me expensive shirt I wanted. I was very angry… But when I noticed the Doctor, I became quiet… no scene there…

Doctor's Verdict: He will be Ok by tomorrow morning. Don't forget scolding him.(I was not supposed to hear this but you can hear certain important things even when the plane in which you are travelling is making noise.)

Enquiry: Continued…

Rector: What were you saying Patnayak? "Bhang is never the answer…

But it does make you forget the question"… and you Malhotra… What did you mean by "I don't have a drinking problem. I drink because I have problems".

I will make sure your problems are only going to increase with this bhang activity of yours…

Are you aware how many parents visited to check up about their sons?

All Of us: pin drop silence.

Rector: 31. (He had a supporting list) (Was he really keeping record? How many fathers? How many mothers? How many other relatives? How many both father and mother? Several questions arose… But who will ask these to him? Again; for 55 students who had bhang, only 31 relatives? Other 24… Were they orphans?

For me, I was among those 24. My house was only 15 minutes walk from hostel. Forget others, even I did not know, when I was in my house and when in hostel! So quick was my to & fro travel. Probably because of this, nobody came… Neither father nor mother… nor elder brother. Frankly fortunately.

30 minutes after having bhang:

I had all sorts of hallucinations… and remembered my entire life again and again… everything was passing like series of visuals.

It is said, "One day or the other, your entire life will pass in front of your eyes… Keep it beautiful"…

I went home only next evening by 8 PM.

My mother asked me, "Where were you for last 3-4 days? Too much study we thought."

Her innocence and faith in her son touched me somewhere.

I decided never to take any bhang in future once I come out of this episode. But how will this episode end? That was the question before me and practically all of us!

Enquiry Part 3 and The Last Part:

Rector: Looking at me… Whose philosophy were you telling? "Reality is an illusion that occurs when you don't have bhang".

Me: W. C. Fields, Sir.

Rector: I don't care. (We knew that. We also would not be bothered. But we were worried about our future in the College.)

Okay, Who was the brain behind this?

All of us: kept quiet.

Rector: Who is the inspiration behind all this?

3 amongst us: Amitabh… Amitabh… (Like in chorus)

(Rector did not smile. He never smiled. At least never in front of students. I don't think he had ever seen a movie. Apart from being rector, he was supervisor for Mechanical workshop. Entire workshop team had only one standard joke for our '*fitting*' [26]project. "Not *fitting…* We can see entire Chemical Engineering building through this."

We had no answer to this comment… Just redo the job… once, twice… till chemical engineering building 'disappears'… Why was this building opposite COE and not some Arts or Commerce college?… Such colleges usually had many more girls at least the visuals would be better)

---

[26] The process of cutting and shaping parts on a custom, craft-production basis to cause them to fit together into an assembly with the proper engineering fit. Part of subject practical in Workshop for Engineering students.

Rector: (Looking at 3 of us) Amitabh what?

and taking notes) Which branch? What is his surname?

3 of us: Hmmmm… No idea, sir.

Rector: We want to fix responsibility… Who is his best friend?

1 of us: Hmm…

Finally I replied: I think Rajesh… (I did not say Khanna)
what if he had heard about Rajesh *Khanna*[27]?

So… no risk.

Rector: Which branch?

(It was difficult to place Amitabh and Rajesh in an
Engineering Branch…)

I said (Representing 3 of us):

I think they are either from Diploma course or Textile
course. We shall let you know sir. After enquiries in 2-3
days time.

Rector: By today evening… Amitabh and Rajesh must be
before me.

We left the interrogation room wondering how to get
Amitabh and Rajesh?

I had an idea! Shall we try *Ram Sharan Don Pandit
Bhangwale*? He said he did a bit role in Don… He may be
knowing Amitabh and even Rajesh.

"No" was the unanimous opinion. "No way… Already
we have enough of trouble"

The Following Week:

We were careful not to cross Rector's path for a week at
least… hoping he will forget… This life where you have to

---

[27]   Superstar in seventies; expired in 2012.

hide from so many things like a thief (*chori – chori chhupke-chhupke jeena*)ruled out any chance of speaking with Neerja, his college-going daughter... Earlier, we had crossed paths twice... once she was wearing blue top and faded jeans and next time white shirt and red skirt... Like I said, there was even a hint of a smile from her once. Some progress was possible I felt... But now with this bhaang reputation, even if she was walking down the stairs, I would not look her in the eyes... out of shame!

Rector Mr. Samant didn't forget anything. But we came to know later, that he was sent on tour for 2-3 days. Also we did not have much contact with Rector since 'Workshop' subject was only for 1st year... We understood Rector had tried to find out from 1st year students... Who are Rajesh and Amitabh the two best friends... of C.O.E.

In the next **45 days**: All of us made good the financial losses of the College.

Luckily, the Bhang matter didn't escalate... (Time Time ki Baat)... Just a matter of time. We were engrossed in submissions, exams...

We wrote our final exam... B.E. (Bachelor of Engineering) and...

It was time to leave both College and Hostel... and it was also the time to hand over Room – keys and possession to Rector...

Showing no expressions, he took the keys from us, checked our records, handed over deposit papers and... unsmilingly asked, "Did you finally find Amitabh and Rajesh?".

I answered: "Sir, we are still trying. We will come back to you, sir. Now that exams are over. We have lot of time now!"

Rector: If you can't find them, bring their photos... Even film-posters will do...

I kept looking at him. He was smiling... Somebody must have told him. Maybe it was his daughter Neerja... *What else had she told him?*

I smiled... Half sure of what was happening... Half scared what if the college wants to fix responsibility on us... "You came to know about Amitabh and Rajesh, sir?"

Rector: Yeah! I had my Intelligence network... I knew the "best friends" Amitabh and Rajesh were not from our college, and the same evening, from my daughter Neerja... I got to know about Amitabh and Rajesh... *But, it was a smart answer...* Neerja laughed at your answer... saying, "What else he could have said? It was a brilliant answer in the circumstances"...

Me: Oh... Sir, sorry for that...

Rector: We are all humans and make mistakes... Neerja said she wanted to talk to you. Did she meet you? She thought you could be brought back on track...

Me: What?... No Sir... Can I meet her now?

(Even now if she can bring me on track, nothing like it!)

Rector: She left for U.K. to study Psychology... but will come back at the end of the semester.

But from now on... no bhang and no indiscipline... I want to see a 'different you' here onwards...

I never had bhang anytime in my life after that...

This bhang episode cost me Rs. 190 /- (share of losses of college property, + Rs. 125/- towards contribution for Bhang), and also… erosion in reputation and most importantly, it cost me Neerja…

Chance of developing friendship with Neerja who had actually laughed at what I had said… Could never have her darshan[28](could never see her) till today after I left the college and the hostel.

That time, with no email and other advanced means of communication, *U.K. and Neerja were way beyond my reach.*

==

---

[28]   Could never see her again but here she is being treated as star and writer her fan.

16

Doctor's Leela

LEELA'S LEELA (CHITTHI AAYI HAI)
(LETTER HAS ARRIVED!)

{And the third chit, which got us our third year marks three days in advance… Can you guess what was written in it?

Like I said, I was dying out of curiosity.

I salute you if you guessed it! It was a…}

(Dedicated to VJTI 1977 Group)

The story is told in reverse flashback style. i.e. most recent flashback first and the oldest flashback, last!

Time: 2013 December 1st week

Amongst all Indian cities 'Delhi atmosphere' is the most politically charged!

I was in Delhi for some work in the first week of December 2013. Polling was on… for the now famous 'Delhi Elections'! 5 pm, 7pm…

Next day, almost half of Delhi population had turned into political pundits! Who will win? There was a 'totawallah' (roadside self proclaimed astrologer with a parrot)) and I thought of asking him about the prediction for Delhi elections. Who will win? He prepared three chits (Congress, AAP and BJP) and quoted a rate of Rs. 100 /- for this prediction! I agreed… Parrot looked at the three chits, came out of his cage and went back… It had refused to predict anything!…

Even the 'totawallah' (owner of parrot) was surprised. "This had never happened before", he said!

Seeing all this, one senior man who was passing by came to me and said, "I can predict!

Rs. 50 /- advance and Rs. 50/- in bank account after prediction proves correct. Can I?"

I accepted… Rs. 50/- for the prediction - chit. He gave me a sealed cover requesting me to open the cover only after the election- results.

I asked him, "Any chance you are aware I am leaving Delhi tonight? I shall watch the results at Mumbai only on TV"

He answered, "No. I am not aware! You can wait in Delhi itself! *but please open the cover only after the results.*"

One day later, after the results were declared, I opened the envelope.

Following was written,"

"Hung assembly.

It is difficult to predict results of elections where important political parties like AAP do not follow the political grammar!

Rs. 50 /- note attached! Returning with thanks!"

I looked at the chit and Rs. 50/- note! What was written was true but can this be called a *prediction*? But like the song goes, "chitthi aayi hai" (Letter has arrived), chitthi arrives only when its time comes!…

I remembered one earlier occasion when I had made use of one such chitthi based on an idea of my friend…

The Year: 2006

I got involved into this second chitthi business, only because of my needless boasting! Some guests had come to our house. It was a Dassera day and the guests could have been happy even with gulabjamun[29] or ice cream as sweet dish. Any decent sweet for that matter. But I was very keen to impress them by my choice of Shrikhand (famous Indian sweet made out of curds) from Jhakaas Restaurant at Dadar. Naturally our guests said, "If you are so keen, we do not mind. Welcome Jhakaas Shrikhand!"

I said, "Give me twenty Minutes" and I rushed to Jhakaas. There was a big queue of about 90 to 100 people standing. This was unexpected! It appeared that several residents of Shivaji Park area were having guests and all of them wanted Shrikhand from Jhakaas! Like me!

With my actor/director friend Puru on scooter, I waited there, not knowing what to do! Some idea stuck Puru and he took me out of the queue. "Let's go out and try something innovative!"

I remembered, *"If you have to break the system, you need to go out of it first"!* He took me out of the queue and up to Sena-Bhawan (Head-quarters of political party Shiv Sena), then he found a paper, actually he chose a paper from several lying there, wrote some words on it, whispered something in my ears, took out his sunglasses, wore them like Cinestar Rajnikant and said "Go. Do as I told you! I will do the rest!"

As if entering for a performance on a stage, Puru entered on that 'stage of Jhakaas Theatre,' where people were collecting packs of Shrikhand one by one and in a queue.

---

[29] Indian sweet made out of mawa from milk

With sunglasses on and like a man on mission, he went straight to the counter where owner / manager was sitting. He asked me to give the envelope and handed it over to the manager. In style!

The dialogue was as under:

Manager: What is this?
Puru: (Looking thro' sunglasses not at him, but at the fan near him which was making noise.)

Please open and read it!

Puru can be very impressive at times! For additional impact, he switched off the fan, hoping that manager would concentrate now only on the chit!

What was written was this,.

"Please hand over 2 Kilo grams of shrikhand to the person carrying this chit!

Required for Balasaheb's guests.

As advised by Sir.

-Sd-

Shakhapramukh. (Branch Manager of Shivsena - Dadar Branch)

N.B. Please collect the money in cash."

Manager read it, read the last line again, took the money first and spoke in a loud voice, "For his guests, Balasaheb[30] needs shrikhand as advised by Sir. Signed by Branch Manager, Shiv sena party"

---

[30]   Balasaheb Thackeray (1926-2012)was an extremely powerful political leader specially in Mumbai City

Nobody in the queue protested. Top 10 people in the queue were anyhow not bothered. They would get their packs in 5-10 minutes. People behind could not get involved because queue was zigzag and long. I got the packs and could continue to boast… "If you have not eaten 'Shrikhand from Jhakaas' in your life, you have practically eaten, nothing!"

My (or are they Balasaheb's?) guests enjoyed shrikhand as advised by 'Sir' on that Dassera day! As a mark of respect, I went to listen to 'Balasaheb and Sir' speaking at Dassera rally of Shiv Sena in the evening.

Again the chitthi had come in time and performed!

I also remembered my first success with one chitthi that performed a miracle, when I walked down the memory - lane!

The year: 1976

By this time, most of us had settled in Engineering. Worries of A.T.K.T. (carried forward papers in arrears) were vanishing, well, almost! Anyway, result day (R-Day) for any student is a day of great curiosity and anxiety, sometimes also like a D-Day.!

One by one, all of us were thinking of scoring First Class now, in order to get a better job!

Ask any student and he will confirm that he shall be glad to have his result 2-3 days prior to the result-day. Who will not? As it is, 3 days before R-day, results are ready with University, they delay it only to catch the 'R-day'. At least we thought so then!

One day, my friend Leela from Electrical branch, informed us that we can get results today, about three days in advance! For that we had to go to University. Her father who was Doctor by profession knew some Kulkarni there and had given her a chit in an envelope. "Once we hand over the chit to Kulkarni we can get the RESULT!", she said.

We went to University and were faced with Problem No. 1: How to locate Kulkarni in the result section? It had a lot of security people outside the door and they would not let us in easily. Somebody (I think Rafique) in the group had an idea, people are bound to come out for lunch. Kulkarni will also come out! We can locate him there at the door!

<u>Leela</u> doubted, "What if he has brought tiffin from home?"

<u>Rafique:</u> Then... hard luck! Let's be positive!

It was nearing 1 PM, and one by one staff-members started coming out from results section. We (six of us)were at the exit gate and were taking turns calling "Kulkarni" to every person coming out in such a manner that only 'That Kulkarni' can hear.

1.00 pm Sharp. We met with success. Kulkarni waved his hand and came to us.

<u>Kul 1</u>: What do you want?
  (We had decided on Reema from our group to speak, being the most charming person in the group!)
<u>Reema:</u> We are 3rd year Engineering Students! Dr. Madgaonkar has given you this chit.
<u>Kul 1</u>: I look after 'Animal Husbandry, Dairies and Fisheries section'.
  I can't help you with engineering results. Sorry!
<u>Reema:</u> No... ok... I mean... but... if you know somebody in engineering section.

<u>Kul 1</u>: I don't meddle with others' work. My parents never taught me that! Sorry. This is Sorry number 2!

Reema was our best bet and here 'this stupid Kulkarni' was brushing her (and us) off casually!

I was about to explain to Kulkarni - 1 that our parents have also taught us exactly the same good things and all of us are only asking for our own results and not anybody else's… So, could he please help us?

But… before I could say anything, he walked past us making a gesture of the numeral '3' with his hand.

<u>Leela</u> explained, "If he means Sorry no. 3 without a word being uttered!

It means danger! Don't try any-more! Let him go.!"

We left him at that!

Security guard had some pity on us! Actually we had given him Vada-Pav(a spicy delicacy famous in Mumbai) to allow us to stand at the door… He consoled, "There are at least three more Kulkarnis. Keep Trying (and *don't forget more of vada - pavs)*"

Turn by turn, we kept trying,… I mean uttering the word 'Kulkarni'!"

1.02 pm. One more man responded to one of the 'Kulkarni' calls.

<u>Kul. 2</u>: Yes?

Reema tried again… Blah… Blah… Blah.

<u>Kul 2</u>: I don't work here! I had myself come to meet somebody to get results of my nephew. Somehow I could enter because of my name… but could not get results.

My man is absent. and sorry, I am not the Kulkarni you want! Try your luck somewhere else!

This was a little more decent and soft '*sorry*' but '*sorry*' again! No hope so far!

1.05 pm

We were losing patience now! Whether we had missed our man Kulkarni? Chitthi was not reaching the proper man.

We kept on saying 'Kulkarni' like a mantra continuously. 50 staff-members had already come out for lunch! At last, one more man responded… this time to Leela!

Kul 3: Oh!… (Pause, looking at all of us)Yes?

For a change, Leela took the lead now. Blah… Blah… ending with 'I am Leela!'

This time response was positive. Kul 3 nodded and took the envelope. Opened. Saw the chit, was about to read it! but said, "OK! Oh Leela, I saw you that small!(Gesture like a small girl) Doctor is your father, is it? Please write all your names, roll numbers and listen… come and meet me at 3pm in the canteen. Don't wait here. It is very strict now-a-days!"

All of us said, "OK. Sure!"

We had no intention of breaking any norms and taking any 'panga'(fight)with anyone!

At 3pm, we got our RESULT! Like movie "Ram Leela", Leela's Leela also worked very well! All of us had passed with decent marks. Some in high 2nd class, and some even in 1st class.

My mind was all the time on the chit and wondered what was written in it, to impress Mr. Kulkarni? After thanking him profusely, I requested, can we get the chit back?

He returned it… saying," yes. Why not? What will I do with it? Give my regards to Doctor! He had cured me completely of my back pain. I am retiring next month but really still feel fit!"(That means in future, no more Leela's Leela for getting results early! Hard Luck!)

In summary, Out of the three chitthis, I received at different times, The first chit of political Pundit was some kind of 'global' statement, which meant nothing, yet it was proved correct because of sound understanding of political grammar!

The second chit was nothing but *twisted truth* and work of a sheer genius of writer / director in terms of *drama* as applied to real life!.

And the third chit, which got us our third year marks three days in advance… Can you guess what was written in it?

Like I said, I was dying out of curiosity. What *Medical grammar* had the Doctor followed? What was Doctor's 'Leela' and what made it work… on Kulkarni?

Will a well-known Doctor write "Please help these students with their marks. Amongst them is also my daughter Leela"

I salute you if you guessed it! *It was… it was… a blank paper. Nothing was written on it*! Just a *plain blank paper!* That's why I call it 'Mother of all the chits'!

Now looking back, I am in still in awe of Dr. Madgaonkar. What a marvellous communication it was?

Words are simply not necessary, when as a Doctor you have cured the patient! Effect of *goodwill is supreme! Political, Dramatic or any other talent cannot compete with it!*

=============*==================*=============

Afterword

I met several characters described in these chapters at different points of time in life. Sixteen stories till now like Bollywood movie '56 till now!' (Ab Tak Chhappan!)

These J.I.M. characters or friends made my life richer with their unique approaches and their personalities.

More the J.I.M. friends that I met... the more I feel that I am re-discovering myself!.

Again and again…

What will happen if I meet all these J.I.M. characters again?… I surely do not rule out this possibility!…

But situations will be different and… new characters may take birth in novel situations. This is true for all of us! We behave differently in different situations at different points of time in our lives.

One thing for sure, I will welcome them and meet them with pleasure, not forgetting to thank them!

=============*==================*============

Acknowledgements

Shekhar Ghate

Dinesh Bobhate

Sanjay Warang

Sharad Jadhav

Uday Godbole

Bharat Madane

Sandeep Kumar

Captain Shrinivasan

Vishwas Shinde

Prakash Shende

Randolph

Pradip Shah

Vivek Kolhatkar

Arun Dharap

Mahesh More

Ajay Nilwarna

Rajiv Bhagwat

Naren Desai

Vandana Kamath

Deepak Nambiar

Rohini Bharadwaj

Muhammad Ishaque

Vilas Mhatre

Anwar Bagdadi

Nittin Keni

Vijay Padhye

Nagesh Hanagodu

Shashikant Deshpande

Shrikrishna Pawar

Mahendra choubisa

Harsh Karande

Chaitanya Kalyanpur

Surya Prakash

Aarti Parekar

Surve

Vickram Ghorpadey

Suresh Patwardhan

Kishor Merchant

Nagesh Pai

and several others whose names I might have inadvertently missed.

To these friends, I have been narrating these stories as they occurred in my life and they were very encouraging and supportive. It is these people who have made this book happen.

Some of them have also "appeared" as characters in some of the stories!

J. I. M.

Jab I Met

(When I Met)

"A Collection of Interesting incidents

With Unforgettable Characters

With Whom I Interacted"

By

SUDHIR VINAYAK JOGLEKAR.